She would win this man's attention if she had to strip down to bare skin to get the job done!

Tess set her glass down on the coffee table with an audible click. She turned and aimed every bit of cleavage she had directly at Jordan's chiseled profile. "Dinner can wait," she said in the most come-hither whisper she could produce.

Jordan turned his head then. And looked. And stared. At last he raised his gaze, inch by inch, until it finally locked with hers. "Are you, by any chance," he said very softly, "trying to seduce me?"

Tess lost her temper. "Of course I'm trying to seduce you! Why else would I go to all this trouble? And *you* have the nerve to tell me you can't wait to eat dinner!"

Hazel eyes wide, Jordan set his glass down with a clunk and rose. His own temper seemed to flare. "Do you know how long I've been ready? Willing, and damn eager, as a matter of fact?"

Now her eyes went wide. "So why didn't you do something?" she asked, her voice quiet.

"Because I thought you weren't ready," Jordan replied.

Tess took a deep breath. "I'm ready."

Dear Reader,

What better way to celebrate June, a month of courtship and romance, than with four new spectacular books from Harlequin American Romance?

First, the always wonderful Mindy Neff inaugurates Harlequin American Romance's new three-book continuity series, BRIDES OF THE DESERT ROSE, which is a follow-up to the bestselling TEXAS SHEIKHS series. *In the Enemy's Embrace* is a sexy rivals-become-lovers story you won't want to miss.

When a handsome aristocrat finds an abandoned newborn, he turns to a beautiful doctor to save the child's life. Will the adorable infant bond their hearts together and make them the perfect family? Find out in *A Baby for Lord Roderick* by Emily Dalton. Next, in *To Love an Older Man* by Debbi Rawlins, a dashing attorney vows to deny his attraction to the pregnant woman in need of his help. With love and affection, can the expectant beauty change the older man's mind? Sharon Swan launches her delightful continuing series WELCOME TO HARMONY with *Home-Grown Husband,* which features a single-mom gardener who looks to her mysterious and sexy new neighbor to spice up her life with some much-needed excitement and romance.

This month, and every month, come home to Harlequin American Romance—and enjoy!

Best,

Melissa Jeglinski
Associate Senior Editor
Harlequin American Romance

HOME-GROWN HUSBAND

Sharon Swan

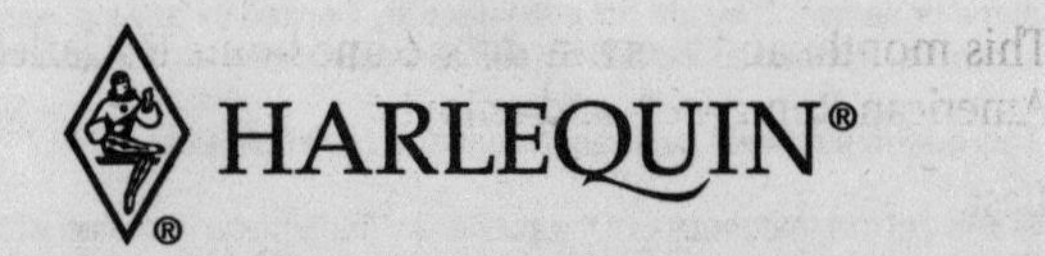

TORONTO • NEW YORK • LONDON
AMSTERDAM • PARIS • SYDNEY • HAMBURG
STOCKHOLM • ATHENS • TOKYO • MILAN • MADRID
PRAGUE • WARSAW • BUDAPEST • AUCKLAND

For my family, the whole wonderful bunch

ISBN 0-373-16928-0

HOME-GROWN HUSBAND

This edition published by arrangement with Harlequin Books S.A.

Visit us at www.eHarlequin.com

Printed in U.S.A.

ABOUT THE AUTHOR

Born and raised in Chicago, Sharon Swan once dreamed of dancing for a living. Instead, she surrendered to life's more practical aspects, settled for an office job, concentrated on typing and being a Chicago Bears fan. Sharon never seriously considered writing a career until she moved to the Phoenix area and met Pierce Brosnan at a local shopping mall. It was a chance meeting that changed her life because she found herself thinking, what if? What if two fictional characters had met the same way? That formed the basis for her next novel, and she's now cheerfully addicted to writing contemporary romance and playing *what if?*

Books by Sharon Swan

HARLEQUIN AMERICAN ROMANCE

912—COWBOYS AND CRADLES
928—HOME-GROWN HUSBAND*

*Welcome to Harmony

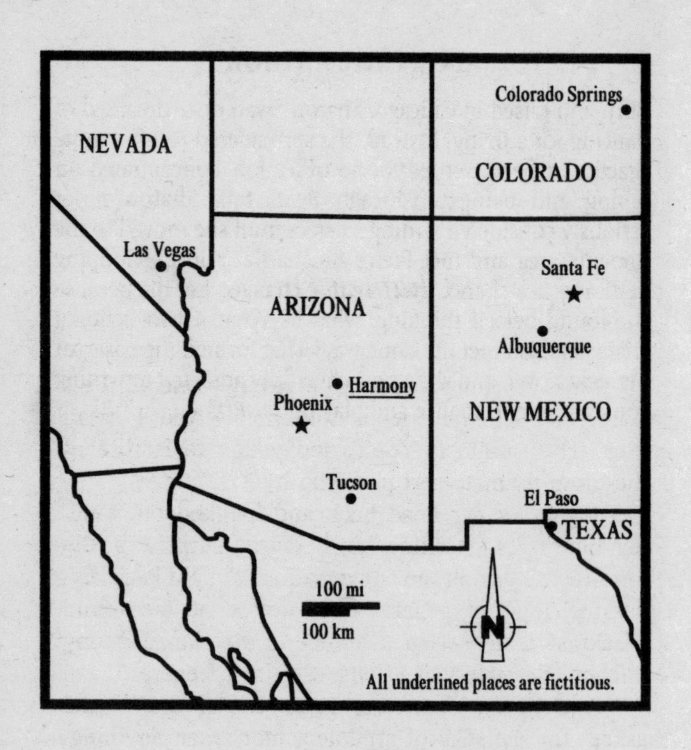
NEVADA
Colorado Springs
COLORADO
Las Vegas
Santa Fe
ARIZONA
Albuquerque
Harmony
Phoenix
NEW MEXICO
Tucson
El Paso
TEXAS
100 mi
100 km
N
All underlined places are fictitious.

Chapter One

"I think it's time you took a lover," one of Tess Cameron's closest friends told her. "And I mean now. This summer. You're too young to let life of the more intimate sort pass you by."

Tess threw her head back and laughed out loud, her blue eyes sparkling with amused surprise at the unexpected turn in the conversation. They'd been discussing men in general over coffee at the round breakfast table set in a corner of her large, sunny kitchen. But this was a long way from general.

"And where do you suggest I find one?" she asked, for the sake of argument more than anything. "You have to admit the pickings are slim in Harmony."

Not that the small city nestled in the low mountains northeast of Phoenix was all that far from Arizona's largest, Tess reflected. Still there was no denying that the majority of males in the immediate vicinity fell into one of three categories when it came to potential lovers for a widow about to turn thirty: too young, too old or too married.

"Slim, but not hopeless," Sally Mendoza maintained with a firm shake of her head that sent her dark shoulder-length hair swinging. "You wouldn't be looking for a husband and daddy replacement, after all, which is admittedly harder to find." Deep brown eyes, slanting up at the tips, narrowed thoughtfully. "At least, I assume you wouldn't."

Tess sipped her coffee, well aware that she'd never raved about her marriage, to Sally or anyone else. "You're right, I'm in no hurry to take another walk down the aisle."

She'd been in too much of a hurry the first time, she recognized in hindsight, too full of youthful ideals and boundless expectations of eternal bliss, to take a step back and consider the wisdom of leaping into a lifetime commitment. Too inexperienced in the ways of the world to know that love alone couldn't conquer all, that two people had to find some common ground, share an understanding of the path they wanted to take in life, one that satisfied them both, before they could share a happy future.

Now she was older, and hopefully wiser.

Not that being married to Roger had been terrible. No, that wasn't true at all. It just hadn't been terribly good after the first year. The only really wonderful thing to come out of it was their daughter, Ali.

"So a lover is what's needed," Sally summed up matter-of-factly.

"Maybe," Tess's sense of honesty had her conceding. She'd been without a man in her life for three years, and her body was increasingly reminding her of that fact. "I can hardly haul one off the street, though—provided there was anything interesting walking around out there to begin with."

Sally lifted one shoulder in a small shrug. "What

about Mr. Mysterious, your new next-door neighbor?''

Tess leaned back in a far-from-new bentwood chair. Despite its age, the faded flowered padding provided a comfortably cozy cushion for her body. Given the choice, she knew she'd take comfort over style any day, even with an unlimited bank account to draw on. That was strictly her preference. The most stylish furniture on the market wouldn't have won a second glance from her, not if it didn't look comfortable.

And even more important than comfort was contentment. To her, it was vital. Rather than taking her good fortune for granted, she routinely thanked her lucky stars that she was content, both with who she was as a person and with the life she'd chosen—even if it might be lacking in one particular area. Then again, having a man around wasn't everything, she reminded herself, although she had to admit to some current curiosity when it came to a certain member of the male species.

''He's mysterious, all right,'' she said, cocking a light brown eyebrow. ''It's been almost a week since he moved in, and I've barely glimpsed him pulling in and out of his garage.''

''Well, sometimes you can tell a lot about people by what they drive.'' Sally tapped a crimson-tipped finger on the glass-topped table. ''Is it a sports car—something sleek, sizzling scarlet, and sexy as sin?''

Tess smiled. ''Sorry to shatter that little fantasy, but it's a fairly late model SUV, probably of the four-wheel-drive variety, and it seems to be black under all the dust.''

''So he's not rich,'' Sally concluded, ''though not poor by any means, given the money they want for those all-terrain numbers, and he's probably been too busy lately to wash it.''

''Or he's been waiting for the wife and six kids to show up and do the job for him,'' Tess tacked on dryly.

Sally finished her coffee and set her mug down. ''Uh-uh. No wife and kiddies. Leslie Hanson told me when I ran into her at the supermarket yesterday that a 'single gentleman' had rented the house her great-aunt left her. A short-term lease, she said.'' A sly grin appeared. ''And it just so happens that your darling child will be gone all summer, visiting her grandparents. I'd say that's fate, Tess.''

''Yeah, right.'' Tess made a face. ''He could easily wind up being the stuff women's nightmares are made of, complete with sweaty palms and a bobbing Adam's apple.''

''Or he could turn out to be your dream man,'' Sally countered as she got to her feet. Today her lush figure was shown to advantage by a navy halter top and walking shorts.

''I don't have a dream man,'' Tess said firmly, rising. Her yellow T-shirt and ancient jeans outlined a slender body that was, she knew, far from lush. She was content with that, as well. Most of the time, at any rate. She just had to stay away from Victoria's Secret catalogs. ''What I have is a daughter I love more than anything in the world, a job I'm crazy about, and definite plans for a good, solid future.''

''Which is absolutely great, and I'm delighted for you. But all of that still won't provide what a full-grown female needs, at least on occasion, in the middle of the night.'' Sally rinsed her mug out in the sink and leaned against the ivory-tile counter. "A lover, on the other hand—"

"Okay, Sal, I get your drift."

"Then give it some consideration," said the mother of cheerfully rowdy, seven-year-old twin boys who was happily wed to a hunk of a husband she blatantly adored—and who clearly returned the favor. "There's no reason to do without certain pleasures when you don't have to. So think about it."

Tess thought about it after Sally left, mulling over her friend's advice as she stared out a curtained kitchen window into the brilliant sunshine so much a part of long summers in the Southwest. Certainly, she had plenty of time to think in the middle of a quiet Saturday morning with Ali away. Too quiet, it seemed, without the sound of well-used running shoes thumping up and down the stairs.

Not that there weren't things to do, she reminded herself. The ever-present laundry, for instance. Vacuuming and dusting, too. Or, in the real-challenge category, she could try to coax the plump cat regally tolerating her presence in her own house into unbending enough to share a companionable hour tending the flowers in the backyard.

But she didn't, she had to admit, feel like tackling even the simplest of those chores. Not today.

Today she felt…restless.

Her body craved something it had done too long without. She couldn't deny that any more than she could magically turn the brown cap of natural curls framing her face into long, straight tresses.

So how did she satisfy that craving? With a willing man, was the obvious answer.

Not a husband, though.

She truly didn't want marriage, not now. But she did want...intimacy, she supposed she could say. More than sex, certainly. Sex had never sent up any skyrockets, not for her. But the closeness that came with it, being held in the grip of strong arms.

Yes, that she couldn't help wanting.

Tess sighed, soft and low. Maybe—just maybe, she thought—it was time to take a lover.

THE LAST THING HE NEEDED was a woman in his life, Jordan Trask told himself. Right now, it was the very last thing. Even thinking along those lines was a mistake.

Too bad that didn't stop him from recalling the special comforts only the opposite sex could supply—something that had been happening more and more and with greater interest, it seemed, since he'd given up a job that, in a perfect world, would never have to be done.

Too bad the world wasn't perfect. And too bad he was having a difficult time deciding how to deal with the future stretching out in front of him like a unmarked road to an unknown place, full of twists and turns. At the moment, that journey held a lot more questions than answers.

Then again, he was lucky, he reminded himself. Damn lucky. He'd gotten out while he could still smile with genuine humor, still laugh on occasion for the sheer pleasure of it. His former profession sometimes destroyed the ability to do both, but he'd survived intact.

He could still feel, really feel, thank God.

And, whether it was wise or not to get involved with a woman at this point, what he felt now was need—the need to touch some silky, smooth skin covering gentle curves, the need to be touched, as well. He was a healthy male in his mid-thirties, after all.

So he had needs. Whether he wanted them or not at this particular time, he had them.

A soft whine drew Jordan's eyes across the width of a homey kitchen to a thick oak door, its upper half etched with squares of sparkling glass topped by a length of ruffled, blue-checked fabric. That the back door led to a spacious, grassy yard continued to be somewhat of a wonder.

Renting a graciously aging house in a quiet neighborhood had been the first of his attempts to experience a whole new way of life. It was the sharpest contrast he could imagine to the series of modern three-room apartments in his past.

Adopting a young, abandoned male basset hound just this morning at the local pound had been another. He'd never had a pet. Not so much as a goldfish, as far as he could remember. And even if he had, this brand-new arrival was a long way from a goldfish.

Oddly enough, though, while the house still felt strange to him, the dog had seemed to settle right in.

Jordan pushed away from the old yet sturdy refrigerator he'd had one shoulder propped against and walked toward the door, making his way over speckled-blue tile. "Time to go out, pal?"

A fast, enthusiastic wag of a skinny tail silently answered the question.

"It's a good thing you're housebroken," he added, meaning every word. Given the life he'd been leading until now, he was far better equipped to handle a coiled rattlesnake primed to strike than a puppy in need of toilet training.

He let the dog out and shoved the door shut—only to wrench it open again with a swift jerk as all hell seemed to break loose outside. The peacefulness all around him seconds earlier, broken only by birds chirping in the tall pines, dissolved in a storm of frantic barking.

What in blazes was going on?

He found out, in a flash, when he stood on the long, covered porch and caught sight of a fat gray cat lounging on the wide top rail of the white, slatted wood fence standing at one side of the yard. The cat gazed down with clear feline disdain as the basset hound defended home territory with a zeal that might have been admirable if it hadn't been deafening.

Before Jordan could try to bring order, the cat had jumped down from the railing and effortlessly landed on the far side. The dog, in an attempt to follow, shoved a quivering black nose through a thin space between the narrow slats, then wiggled back and roamed the length of the barrier that foiled him, growling nonstop.

"Give it up, pal, it's over," Jordan called, thinking it was—until the dog began to claw a path under the fence at a spot toward the rear of the yard where the ground had eroded.

Jordan noticed that slight dip for the first time. And it was too late.

Dirt flew. The dog squeezed through.

Then all hell broke loose again.

It was a woman's startled cry that sent Jordan racing headlong toward the chest-high fence. He scaled it with little trouble, landed flat on booted feet with a soft thump, and steeled himself, more than half expecting to find a silver-haired matron on the verge of the vapors, dead certain he'd rather deal with a hundred of the meanest rattlers ever born than a single bout of hand-flapping hysterics.

It turned out he didn't need to.

At least he figured as much when he found a far-from-matronly woman crouched down on jean-clad knees in the grass beside a two-story, wood-framed house very much like the one he'd rented. His was painted blue. This one was white.

And the woman was clearly seeing red.

With gloved hands clenched at her sides, and sporting a thunderous frown, she viewed a disaster in progress right in front of her as Jordan's canine companion chased a furry target straight down the middle of a long flower bed.

This lady wasn't hysterical, he told himself. Or upset. Even irritated wouldn't begin to cover it. She was, in a word, furious.

Still braced for action, he gave some thought to making a fast return trip over the fence and leaving the hound to face the consequences. What had prompted him to think he needed a pet, anyway, he wondered. Sheer insanity, he was beginning to believe.

Then the choice to stay or retreat vanished when the cat suddenly changed course and headed straight for him, followed in a heartbeat by the dog. Both made a swift circle around him, then headed back and retraced their path through the flower bed to complete the destruction before racing off toward the far side of the house.

Rather than following their progress, a sharp, clear blue gaze pinned Jordan where he stood. He'd always been a sucker for blue eyes. Usually they'd been attached to a tall, cool blonde. As the owner of these eyes surged to canvas-shod feet, he noted she was neither tall nor short. Just about average height for a full-grown woman, he decided.

Her figure was neat and trim, her hair a shiny cap of honey-brown curls. Her face was more heart shaped than round. And if she wore makeup, it wasn't obvious, even in stark sunlight. The flattering color on her cheeks might be due to sheer fury, but the rosy shade of her lips seemed natural.

Why he should think of *wholesome* to describe her, he couldn't say, especially since she looked ready to wrap her hands around someone's throat. Probably his.

"Is that your dog?" Even brisk with anger, her voice came out as soft as the grassy ground under his boots.

"If I say no, will you let me live?" He folded his arms across his chest, grateful she wasn't shouting the place down, and tried for a wry smile.

Steps away from him, Tess stilled completely for a moment. The question, and the smile, had taken her off guard.

No one had a right to be that damn attractive was her first thought as she found herself staring frankly. Her second thought was that no one would ever judge this man as ordinary. Even dressed in well-worn denim, he made one heck of an impact. *And no one would ever know you had a brain in your head right now* was her next reflection, directed squarely at herself, as reality returned and had her blinking.

So what if a broad-shouldered, lean-muscled, flat-out devastating male, the type of man she'd never, by any stretch of the imagination, expected to appear in her backyard, suddenly had?

So what if he was tall, dark, and not quite classically handsome, but close enough?

So what if that crooked smile rattled her pulse and the hazel eyes above it seemed to bore right into hers?

So *what?* She was supposed to be livid.

"I'd say your survival could well hinge on getting that animal out of here," she told him, clipping the words.

"I'll do my best," he hastened to assure her, his voice deep and low, rough around the edges, but not at all unpleasant to the ear. "I hope your cat's okay."

Tess let out a breath. "It's your dog that will probably be in trouble when Roxy gets tired of fooling around."

As if to prove that statement, a gray streak of fur came zipping around the house with a brown-and-white blur in hot pursuit. All at once, the cat spun around in midair, hissing, and swatted the hound flat on the nose with some well-placed claws. Then, to the tune of canine yelps, the victor leaped back on the fence rail and calmly stretched out, acting as if nothing unusual in the least had happened.

"Guess I don't have to worry about Roxy," the man muttered as the dog, head bent, trotted over to stand beside him. "Had enough?" he asked, looking down, and got a soft whine in reply.

Once again those hazel eyes met hers. This time, Tess was ready for the jolt and managed to view him coolly. He'd never know, she thought with satisfaction, that her pulse was still none too steady. In fact, at the moment she was sure he looked a lot more uncomfortable than she did.

"I suppose I should introduce myself before I take the culprit away. I'm Jordan Trask. I rented the place next door and moved in a few days ago."

"I knew someone had moved in," she offered in return. *But I never anticipated anyone like you.*

"I really am sorry about the flowers," he added, sounding as if he meant just that.

Tess tossed a rueful glance over her shoulder. There was little chance to save anything, she knew. The damage was too complete. "I'll have to replant," she thought out loud.

"I'll gladly pay for whatever you need to get the job done. And I'd be willing to help, if you'll let me."

Tess slowly swung her head back around and took a moment to consider her options. Three quickly came to mind.

She could tell Jordan Trask to just get lost—even in a nice way, if she wanted to be polite.

She could also accept his money and decline the assistance—again diplomatically, if she cared to.

Or she could go with the final choice and take advantage of an unexpected opportunity to get to know her new neighbor.

Sure, he was drop-dead attractive. Probably no woman who could see past her nose would disagree with that judgment. But something less appetizing could still lurk under that mouthwatering exterior. And she might never find out for certain, unless…

Tess squared her shoulders. "I'm Tess Cameron. And I'll take you up on that offer."

He raised a dark eyebrow. "The one to reimburse you, or the one to help."

"Both."

MAYBE HE SHOULD HAVE ADMITTED that he didn't know squat about gardening. Then again, Jordan thought as he carefully scooped rich black dirt with a small metal trowel, Tess Cameron might very well have told him thanks, but no thanks when it came to helping. For some reason, he'd been determined not to let that happen, not if there was any chance he could spend more time with her.

Something about the woman now crouched at his side drew him. What exactly, he was still trying to figure out. Whatever it was, physical attraction played a major part. He was dead certain of that.

They were all but hip to hip, and he was fully aware of the scant space between them, right down to the barest inch. If he moved, just a little, he could touch her. And he had no business touching her, he knew. Or thinking what he was thinking.

He'd be far better off keeping his mind on what he was doing—or at least attempting to do.

Thankfully, he hadn't been useless up to this point. No one could deny he'd done a thorough job of hauling the trampled mess out of Tess Cameron's flower bed and dumping it in the trash while she retrieved a fresh batch of plants. That part had been easy. Even easier was reimbursing her—and noting the absence of any rings, wedding or otherwise, as she took his money with one hand and offered a receipt with the other.

Now came the hard part. Jordan frowned down at the hole he'd created, wondering if he should stop or keep on digging. Who knew?

"That needs to be a little larger," his companion pointed out, glancing over at his effort.

"Right." He dug a bit deeper and wider, then

aimed for a casual tone. "That should do it, wouldn't you say?"

"Looks good. I think some snapdragons would go well there."

She returned to her own digging then, clearly expecting him to get on with it. Great. Jordan turned his head and studied the bunched flowers in a variety of shapes and colors lined up behind him. What the hell did a snapdragon look like? He recognized the roses. Everything else was a mystery.

"I like lots of yellow," she added. "It makes things bright and cheerful."

Yellow. That might be a clue. There were two varieties of mostly yellow flowers—tall, thin ones, and shorter, rounder ones. Figuring he had a fifty-fifty chance, he went with the shorter version.

"No, not the marigolds," she told him when he set his choice in front of him. "Snapdragons."

"Right."

He replaced his gamble with the taller yellow version and decided luck was with him this time when she offered no objection. While she reached behind her for another plant, he carefully removed his from its plastic container and placed it in the hole. He held it with one hand and cautiously spread dirt over the roots.

Then he let it go and watched it fall over, toppling like a felled tree in the forest.

Swallowing a curse, he slid a look at his companion out of the corner of his eye and saw a thoughtful frown form as he straightened the plant.

"You haven't done much gardening, have you?"

"No." Which was, he told himself, the complete truth.

Her frown deepened. ''How much have you done?''

He resisted the urge to sigh. The jig was up, he knew, because he wouldn't outright lie to her. ''None—until now,'' he admitted, turning to look straight at her.

The frown remained. ''And you offered to help me anyway. Why?''

''My dog did the damage, so it's only fair that I help.'' Again it was the truth. Maybe not the whole truth, but his conscience wouldn't bother him about it.

Gradually her frown faded as her lips curved, slowly and wryly. ''Then I guess it's time for a lesson...Jordan,'' she said, using his name for the first time.

He released a quiet breath and offered silent thanks that she was taking it well. He'd seen her fuming, and was in no hurry to repeat the experience. The curve of his mouth matched hers. ''I'd say you're right...Tess.''

''Okay.'' She set aside the container of tiny blue flowers she held and bent over the plant he still supported. ''The trick is to pack the dirt gently but firmly around the roots.'' She demonstrated with gloved hands, close enough now to allow him a long whiff of a crisp, fresh fragrance he was sure came from her and not the flowers. Done with her project seconds later, and too soon, as far as everything male inside him was concerned, she leaned away again and sat back on her haunches.

''You can let it go now.''

He did, and the plant stood straight and tall.

"It's not difficult once you get the hang of it," she said. "My eight-year-old daughter is already a pro."

That news brought him up short. "Your daughter? I haven't seen a child around." Then again, he hadn't seen this woman either, until he'd stormed over the fence.

"Ali's spending the summer with my parents. They live in San Diego."

And where's Ali's father? He didn't voice the question, yet something in his expression must have made it plain. At least he figured that was the case when she said, "My husband died a few years ago." Her own expression sobered with the words.

"I'm sorry." The reply came automatically, but he meant it, nonetheless.

"Roger was killed in a car crash." She hesitated, as if she could have gone on to say more, then silently picked up the spray of flowers she'd put aside and began to plant them. By the time she finished, her smile, or a ghost of one, was back. "We went through some tough times, Ali and I, but we're doing fine now. We have a good life, and I have a job I love."

"What kind of job?"

Her smile widened as she started to dig another hole. "This kind, actually. I work for Zieglers Landscaping Service. If things go as planned, I'll own the business before the year is out. Hank and Violet Ziegler, the current owners, are getting ready to retire and take things easier, and they've offered to sell it to me. The day it becomes Cameron Landscaping, I'll be celebrating—big time." She reached around and retrieved the plant he'd put back earlier.

Marigolds. Jordan remembered the name even as he considered what Tess Cameron had just told him.

Although she'd lost her husband, this woman was clearly looking forward to the future. She couldn't be more than thirty—probably less—yet she had her life mapped out, at least career-wise. She knew exactly where she wanted to go and fully expected to find satisfaction in the path she'd chosen.

He couldn't help but envy her.

"I take it you know all about growing things," he said in a bid to keep the conversation going.

She shook her head. "Not everything, not nearly, but I've learned my share during the years I've spent working on lawns all over the city."

Leaning forward, he ignored a lone bee that buzzed by and scooped out another trowel's worth of dirt. "So why don't you tell me more?"

She did, and he in turn did his best to keep up with the flow of information. Flowers not only came in all shapes, colors and sizes, there were apparently different types, as well. Annuals. Perennials. Biennials.

And he'd be willing to bet none of them smelled as good as the woman beside him, he thought at one point. Still, he found himself interested, even though he knew that just yesterday, if anyone had told him he'd not only be listening to a lecture on gardening, but on his knees planting roses at the same time, he'd have called them flat-out crazy.

Time passed swiftly, and before it seemed possible they were finished. Jordan was bending over to retrieve a shovel they'd used when his instructor said, "I've been talking about my livelihood long enough. What do you do for a living?"

Not anything he wanted to discuss. Although he realized he should have expected it, the question had him stilling completely for an instant as he debated how to answer.

Standing beside him, Tess's gaze sharpened as she caught that sudden total lack of movement before Jordan slowly straightened. Her question had been natural enough, she told herself, but it seemed to have made an impact, however well concealed. Another second passed before she got a reply.

"I don't do much of anything these days," he told her in the same casual tone he'd used for much of the afternoon. "Exploring my options, I guess you could say."

And what did you do up till now? She couldn't help wondering, thinking that whatever it was, it had surely not been a run-of-the-mill job. Sharing several companionable hours doing something as simply satisfying as flower tending hadn't changed her mind about Jordan Trask. No one would ever judge him to be ordinary...including her.

She waited a moment for him to say more. He said nothing, so she turned and started for the garage with an armload of small garden tools. He followed, carrying a shovel in one hand and a fat sack of mulch with the other. Once inside, he glanced around him. "Where do you want the sack?"

"Against the wall, on the other side of the truck." She watched as he walked in near silence around her white pickup, asking herself if anyone could move that quietly on solid concrete unless they'd been trained in the art. For a moment, her attention was so fixed on him that she didn't even notice the short metal rake slipping from the pile she held, not until it hit the hard floor with a clatter.

In a flash, the man she viewed dropped the sack

and whipped around to face her, hazel eyes narrowed and broad shoulders braced for what might come next. He looked, she thought, like a shot had just been fired, rather than a tool clattering.

Like a shot. All at once Tess got a good inkling of what Jordan Trask had done in the past. Her gaze locked with his. ''Are you ex-military, or ex-police?''

As he released a lengthy breath, she could all but see him forcing himself to relax. And then he spoke so softly that the words barely reached her.

''Neither. I'm ex Border Patrol.''

Chapter Two

Border Patrol. The words repeated in Tess's mind. It was a long way from ordinary, even quite possibly dangerous work. She didn't know any more than the average person, she supposed, about what was actually involved. But she knew that much.

No wonder, she told herself. No wonder he seemed a bit larger than life, as though he'd just stepped from the pages of an action novel. He'd probably seen plenty of action.

And now he had apparently chosen to give it up, let it all go, for reasons she certainly had no business asking him about. Still she couldn't hold back one question. "How did you wind up in Harmony?"

He bent to lift the sack, then met her eyes again. "I saw an article in a travel magazine at a dentist's office a while back. It was on bed-and-breakfasts in this area, and one of the pictures was an aerial photo of this place, with the sun shining down on it." He paused for a beat. "I've got to admit it seemed a little like heaven to me."

It must have, after the sights he'd no doubt seen hundreds of miles to the south. She could understand that, even though Tess knew the city she'd lived in for most of her life wasn't heaven. She'd learned that the hard way when—

"So I figured I'd come and check it out," Jordan added, breaking into memories she was far from reluctant to let go. "It didn't take me long to decide I wanted to spend some time here." With that, he turned away and placed the sack where she'd indicated. "What about the shovel?"

She reached down and retrieved the rake from the floor. "It goes in the storage box at the back."

The tools were scarcely put away when thunder rumbled in the distance. "Guess I won't have to water the new plants," Tess said as they left the garage. The coming rain was hardly a surprise. Late-day, wind-whipped storms rolled in regularly during the summer months in Harmony, sometimes disappearing almost as quickly as they blew in.

The thick dark hair at the nape of his neck barely brushed his shirt collar as Jordan gazed up at a sky that was quickly turning murky. "I'd better be going. I should probably let the dog out to do his duty before it starts coming down. I'll keep him on a leash until I make sure he can't get through the fence again and create another crisis."

Tess's lips quirked in a small smile. "I doubt he'll be giving Roxy any more trouble."

"If he's smart, he won't."

"Is he smart?"

"I don't know, but I expect I'll find out." Jordan brushed his palms on his Levi's. "We just met today. I adopted him at the pound this morning."

And he didn't look all that certain he'd done the wise thing, she had no trouble noting. It only made her smile widen. "What's his name?"

With a slight shake of his head, Jordan said, ''Beats me. The people at the pound thought he was abandoned because someone couldn't, or didn't want to, take care of him anymore.''

''Then you'll have to rename him.''

He frowned, aiming a thoughtful glance at the house he'd rented, where his new pet awaited his return. ''I've never named a dog before. What, ah, do you think I should call him?''

It was her turn to slowly shake her head. ''It doesn't matter what I think, not really. He's yours now, Jordan. You should name him.''

Once again, his gaze met hers. ''Do you suppose he could come over and visit sometime—if he behaves himself?''

Her heart picked up a heavy beat, right along with her pulse, because she knew by the abruptly probing glint in his eye what he was really asking. She didn't even consider saying no. ''You can both come over,'' she said, and managed to keep her tone light.

He grinned then—an all-out grin, not just a smile—and she couldn't stop her breath from catching at the sight, couldn't help but wonder if he had any idea how knockout sexy it was. ''We just might take you up on that invitation,'' he told her, his gaze still steady on hers.

She barely held on to her composure until he looked away and started toward the fence separating their yards. ''You can go around the front, you know,'' she called after him.

''This is just as easy,'' he threw back over his shoulder. And it was, for him. Within seconds, he effortlessly landed on the other side and turned to wave goodbye. The grin—that devilishly sexy grin—was still in place.

TESS WATCHED through a side window of her kitchen as man and dog made their way around the yard, one holding a long black leash, the other sniffing a path over bright green grass. Without a doubt, the dog needed his owner, she thought, needed to be cared for as any pet would. For some reason, though, she was beginning to believe that this particular owner just might need what the dog could provide every bit as much. It should have seemed a little ridiculous that someone who appeared so confidently self-sufficient could genuinely benefit from some unconditional canine devotion.

But it didn't seem at all ridiculous. Not to her. Not after the time spent with her new neighbor.

Jordan Trask had come to Harmony seeking something. Of that, she was sure. Less clear, was exactly what he sought. Sheer peace, maybe. Some quiet time to decide what he'd do next after leaving a job that would have been anything but peaceful.

It might well be the case, she reflected, recalling their conversation. He'd seen a postcard-perfect photo in a magazine, and the image had come to mind at a time when he'd needed to get away. Yes, that could very well be it.

Not that it was any of her business, Tess reminded herself as the phone on a nearby wall jangled. She stepped back from the window and picked up the cream-toned receiver on the second ring. Her daughter's voice greeted her.

"How's it going, Mom?"

Breaking into a smile, Tess leaned against the

kitchen counter. ''Just fine, pumpkin. What have you been up to?''

''Lots. Grandma took me to the beach today. We had a good time, even though Grandpa didn't go. He wanted to stay home and watch a baseball game instead. Tomorrow Gram and I are going to the zoo. She asked Grandpa to go, too, but he says there's another game on TV.'' Ali issued a dramatic sigh. ''I think Grandpa's turning into a couch potato.''

''Sounds like it,'' Tess agreed, remembering a time when her father had loved being outdoors as much as she did now.

''Just between us—'' Ali's voice dropped to a confidential pitch ''—Grandma told him when she probably thought I wasn't listening that if he keeps on acting like his butt is glued to the recliner, she's gonna get fed up one of these days and do something drastic.''

Tess's smile grew, because she had no trouble imagining her mother delivering those words in a familiar no-nonsense tone. Glenda Fitzgerald was a woman who could tell it like it was, and didn't hesitate to do so if she felt the occasion demanded it.

''What do you suppose Gram meant by something *drastic,* Mom?''

''Who knows?'' Tess pursed her lips. ''Maybe cutting the cord on the TV. Or fixing fish for dinner every night.''

''Aha,'' Ali said wisely. ''Gram and I like fish, but Grandpa doesn't.''

Chuckling, Tess replied, ''Exactly, pumpkin. Your grandfather would be making his own dinner, which probably falls in the drastic category, at least as far as he's concerned. He'd be mumbling and grumbling all over the place.''

Ali giggled. The sound was music to Tess's ears. Her daughter had gone through some dark days after Roger died, but the shadows had long since faded, thank heavens. ''Tell me what else you've been up to,'' she urged, and, as expected, Ali launched into an eager explanation.

With a promise to call during the week, Tess hung up the phone minutes later and returned to the window. The first big drops of warm rain hit with soft pings and slid their way down the glass as she looked out at the now empty yard next door.

He was gone. But not forgotten. Even a lively conversation with her much-loved child hadn't pushed her neighbor completely from her mind. No, he was still there. Those dark-lashed eyes, that chiseled mouth, the knockout grin.

And the powerful body. She couldn't deny that she remembered every impressive inch of it, and she couldn't say that she'd object to seeing more. Because she wouldn't.

As a lover, Jordan Trask would be ideal.

Even as that thought bloomed, she was struck by exactly how right it seemed. Not for just any woman, but for her. In every way she could imagine, this man fit the part to a tee.

Physically, she was attracted to him. Just kneeling beside him in a flower bed was the most exciting thing she'd done in years, at least as far as everything female inside her was concerned. Her pulse still hadn't returned to normal. Not quite. Not yet. She wondered how long it would take.

Emotionally, he attracted her, as well. Watching

him warily bond with his new pet had tugged at her heartstrings, she couldn't deny. And the fact that the dog clearly wasn't wary spoke volumes. Deep down, he was a good man—one she could come to respect, given the chance. Every instinct she had said so.

And, added to all of the above, one more thing about him held great appeal. Right now, at this point in her life and circumstances being what they were, it was the icing on the cake.

Jordan Trask would be a temporary lover.

Temporary, because she didn't for one minute believe that he would settle down in Harmony. He'd come here to find something, probably a solid strategy for what to do next, and having found it, he would move on. Men well acquainted with the thrill of danger didn't prop their boots up on a porch railing in peaceful surroundings and contentedly watch the world go by. Not for any *real* length of time.

So he would go. And if they did become lovers, when it was over there would be no uncomfortable aftermath. That was one of the difficulties of living in a smaller city, Tess knew. If she set her sights on someone local, they'd be running into each other long after the affair had run its course—whether they wanted to or not.

Far better, she believed, to choose someone who was exciting on one level, admirable on another, and…temporary.

Oh, yes. It would be ideal.

He was here for the summer. Her daughter was happily occupied elsewhere. Perfect.

And what made her think he would even consider it?

Tess shook her head as that thought hit home, and

soon chided herself for pure foolishness. Here she was, she reflected with a rueful twist of her lips, flirting with the idea of an intimate relationship with her new neighbor, when he hadn't so much as flirted with her, not really. Time for a reality check, she concluded, turning away from the window.

The man in question had done nothing to launch her mind down the particular path it had taken. Nothing but grin at her and waggle an invitation to possibly come over again—which was hardly enough to mean anything. After all, Tess told herself as she started for the laundry room, larger-than-life men hardly made a habit of getting involved with down-to-earth women.

Did they?

THE FLOWERS INVADED Jordan's dreams that night. Rainbow-colored and brightly scented, they marched straight into his imagination, a brilliant parade of blooms in endless shapes and sizes. Roses. Snapdragons. Marigolds. And a legion more he still couldn't put a name to.

In his mind, he walked in a huge garden at the height of a sultry summer day, gazing around him as he made his way down a narrow cobblestone path carved into a sea of lush green grass. The goal foremost in his thoughts was to reach a certain place, to find a certain…something. The knowledge of exactly what, eluded him keeping a quick, enticing step ahead to remain just beyond his grasp.

But he was dead sure he had to find it.

So he kept on going, while birds chirped softly in the background and warm wind rustled a thousand leaves.

And then he came to a sharp twist in the winding path and saw a woman seated on a plain wooden bench in a small clearing. Everything inside him clenched at the sight, because she wore nothing but a yellow rosebud tucked behind one ear. He knew that for a certainty, despite the fact that only her face was completely clear to him, as if a filmy veil cloaked the rest of her body from his gaze.

She made no attempt to cover herself, showed no surprise at his appearance. Rather, her eyes welcomed him, blue as the sunlit sky above, as he approached. And all at once he realized he'd found what he'd been looking for.

Swiftly on the heels of that knowledge came a surge of want. He wanted many things, wanted them badly and wanted them soon. But most of all at that moment, he wanted to kiss the woman who awaited him.

As if well aware of his thoughts, she rose in one smooth motion, spread her arms and slid them around his neck without hesitation when he finally stood beside her. Then she pressed her lips to one side of his jaw and feathered her tongue over his cheek. He longed for her mouth under his, craved a deep, hard taste. Yet he found himself willing to wait, because what she was doing felt so good. So warm. So...moist.

So arousing.

Or it would have been, if something hadn't prompted him to slit an eye open. He quickly discovered that Tess Cameron was nowhere in sight. But he was indeed being licked.

By a dog.

"What the hell!" Jordan shot straight up in the

brass double bed, sending the white sheet tumbling to his waist. He wore nothing beneath it, preferring bare skin to bunched pajamas when it came to nightwear. And as far as morning wake-up kisses were concerned, he'd take sweet, human female over damp canine any day.

"Don't ever do that again," he grumbled, frowning down at his new pet. A pet still lacking a name, he reminded himself. Not that he hadn't given it his best shot. He had. But nothing seemed to fit.

The dog, looking totally unrepentant, calmly returned his master's gaze, wet tongue lolling to one side and black eyes gleaming in the dim early sunlight slanting through the sheer blue bedroom curtains.

"It might be easier to get my point across if I had a clue what to call you." Jordan punched up a pillow and leaned back against it. "Maybe I should leave the whole thing up to you."

A soft pant began at that statement, appearing to agree.

He shrugged. "Okay, let's give it a try. How does Spot strike you?"

No reaction at all, not this time.

"No dice, huh? How about Rover? Lad? Sparky?"

Nothing.

"Buster? Rex? Fang?"

Zip.

He lifted a hand and ran it through his sleep-mussed hair. "You'd better not be too picky, pal. I may reach the end of my rope, and you'll wind up with a name as plain as Smith or Jones."

A sudden lively bark split the early-morning quiet and sent Jordan's brows climbing. "Are you telling me you want to be called something like *Jones?*"

A second bark and some fast tail wagging gave him his answer. "All right, who am I to argue the point? If Jones works for you—it's Jones." Jordan flicked the sheet aside, rose and headed for the bathroom off the upstairs hallway.

At the sound of yet another eager bark, he tossed a glance over his shoulder and found the dog now eyeing the warm spot on the bed he'd just left. "Don't even think about it, Jones."

Sighing, Jones dropped his chin to the sea-toned carpet and placed his head on his paws.

Jordan's mouth curved in a satisfied smile. "I see we now understand each other."

But what he didn't understand, he had to admit as he stood under the shower's pulsing spray and soaped himself down, was why he'd had that dream. Sex had something to do with it, of course. Without the dog getting into the act, who knew where that fantasy would have ended. Maybe with two naked bodies stretched out on the grass in the middle of that garden.

Yeah, his libido was involved, all right. But he doubted it was only his libido. Other aspects of the dream had been too strong. What he'd wanted went beyond a willing woman, an anonymous face with a soft-skinned body.

No, he'd wanted one woman in particular.

And he'd best stay away from her until he decided where to go from here. If, that was, he decided to do anything beyond aiming a friendly wave over the fence for the rest of the summer. Logic told him he should do exactly that and concentrate on the gaping hole in his future. Too bad certain parts of him weren't feeling especially logical.

Then again, the woman in question might choose

to toss no more than an occasional wave his way. Jordan frowned as it occurred to him that his neighbor might already have a man in her life, given the fact that she'd been a widow for a few years. For some reason, that thought didn't sit well, but there it was. It would be foolish to go off half-cocked before he got a better handle on the whole thing.

So, taking everything into account, he was a lot better off staying away from Tess Cameron, at least for the time being. With that conclusion, Jordan stepped from the shower and reached for a fluffy blue towel. He tried not to dwell on the fact that it all but matched the shade of the eyes belonging to the vision in his dream, tried not to imagine how her touch might feel as he rubbed his body dry.

Tried...and failed.

"SO THEN WHAT HAPPENED?"

"He jumped back over the fence. And maybe straight out of my life."

Sally, once again seated at the breakfast table in her friend's kitchen, lifted a brow right along with her coffee mug. "Does that mean you haven't laid eyes on him since?"

"Not exactly. I saw him on Sunday morning nailing up some plywood boards where his dog managed to get through." Tess leaned back in her chair. "He, ah, didn't have a shirt on."

"Oh, my." Sally blew out a breath and began to fan herself with one hand. "Judging by what you've already told me, that must have been quite a sight."

With the vivid memory of a hair-darkened chest still firmly etched in her mind, Tess could hardly disagree. "It was." She took a hefty sip of coffee.

"Then, that afternoon, he mowed the lawn—still minus a shirt and this time wearing denim cutoffs instead of jeans."

Fanning faster, Sally said, "And the lower half was as impressive as the upper, right?"

"Right." So impressive, Tess thought, that she'd been hard-pressed not to pant at the whole picture as she watched Jordan Trask through the kitchen window. His obvious effort to master the mysteries of the old-fashioned gas mower hadn't dimmed the impact one watt, even before he'd solved the puzzle and proceeded to get the job done.

Sally stopped fanning. "And you didn't find something—anything—to do outside so you could talk to him again?"

"No."

"Why?"

A good question, Tess had to concede. It would have been nice to have a clear answer. As it was, she shrugged. "Maybe I just wasn't ready for another chat." *Or maybe, after getting an eye-widening look at that body, I felt even more foolish for so much as considering the possibility of an affair with a man who'd draw drop-dead-gorgeous women like a magnet.*

Sally's sudden smile was sly. "Do I detect the patter of cold feet?"

"No, you do not," Tess replied briskly. "If I'd wanted to strike up a conversation with Jordan Trask last Sunday, I would have damn well done it."

"And how about the rest of the week?"

Tess smiled her own smug smile. "I only caught glimpses of him coming and going in his car, so there was no chance to talk to him."

"But if he takes you up on that invitation and stops by this weekend," Sally countered, "there'll be no reason not to chat up a storm."

Tess set down her empty mug and aimed for a breezy tone. "Sure, if he shows up on my doorstep, I'll be my usual friendly, neighborly self."

But it wouldn't surprise her if the man in question never showed up. And if he chose not to, she would be content with that decision, Tess told herself.

Except maybe in the middle of the night, an inner voice tacked on, and she knew it had a point.

At midnight, when she'd already found her mind wandering to the moonlit house next door, contentment might be hard to come by. Hard, but not impossible.

"As intriguing as this subject is," Sally said with a soft sigh, "I'd better head home soon. Ben's probably close to done with the yard work by now and then we have to start setting up tables for the barbecue tonight."

Tess brightened at the reminder that for the coming evening at least, she'd have plenty to occupy her mind. The annual party held in the sprawling backyard of the Mendoza home had become a summer tradition in Harmony. It was also good customer relations on their part. With Ben being a C.P.A. and Sally serving as his assistant, tax time had clients from all over town visiting the business they ran from their house.

"I can almost taste those Texas-style beef ribs now, Sal. Should I be there around seven?"

"Uh-huh. As usual, things start when the sun goes down." Again a sly smile broke through. "You're welcome to bring a date, you know. There'll be plenty of food—even for a big man with a major appetite.''

Tess shook her head, well aware of Sally's choice for the role. ''I believe I'll take a pass.'' She pushed away from the table and got to her feet. ''On the other hand, if you don't pass on another cup of coffee, Ben and the kids may have the tables set up by the time you get there.''

''Excellent thinking,'' Sally decided. ''I can show up in time to supervise the decorations, which, by the way, will not include crepe paper.'' She shuddered. ''I learned my lesson last year after that thunderstorm blew through and left sopping mounds of it behind. This year, I'm sticking with strictly waterproof material.''

''Good plan.'' Tess started for the coffeepot on the counter, then halted in midstride when the front doorbell rang. ''I wonder who that can be.''

Sally arched a skillfully shaped brow. ''Maybe it's *him.*''

Him.

Tess's pulse picked up a beat even as she calmly shoved the bottom edge of her striped camp shirt more firmly into the waistband of her jeans. ''Not likely. It's probably somebody selling something. Saturday mornings are great for that kind of thing.''

''Why don't you find out?'' Sally suggested, rising. ''Meanwhile, I'll pour us both another cup of coffee.''

''Okay.'' Tess turned on the heel of one canvas sneaker, left the kitchen and walked down the hall, telling herself that it was ridiculous to feel this nervous about doing something so everyday normal as answering the door. It could well be a neighborhood kid selling candy to finance a school project, or an elderly resident seeking volunteers at the senior center. It could be anyone, she thought as she opened the door.

But it wasn't anyone, she learned after one look at the person dressed in faded denim standing on the doorstep.

It was him.

"Hello, Tess," he said in the low, rough voice she remembered all too well. "We decided to take you up on that invitation."

We? It took her another moment and a second, more thorough look to notice that his newly adopted pet stood beside him, long ears brushing the white slats of a narrow porch floor being eagerly sniffed.

"Hello...Jordan." She had to say more than that, she knew. She just didn't know what. Finally she settled on action and gestured a welcome. "Come on in."

He stepped forward with a slight tug on the dog's leash, and spoke again as Tess closed the door behind them. "Is this a good time? I don't want to disturb you if you're busy."

"It's a great time." A soft voice drifted down the hall from the spot where Sally leaned in the kitchen doorway, mug in one hand and a wide smile curving red-shaded lips that all but matched her figure-hugging jumpsuit. "We gals were just having some coffee."

"Why don't you join us?" Tess suggested, her brain kicking in at last.

His crooked smile appeared. She remembered that, too. Not to mention the thick dark hair, the keen hazel eyes and the rest of the whole potent package. She doubted she'd ever totally forget it.

"That's fine with me," he said, and the basset hound seemed to second the statement with a quiet woof. "Sounds like Jones agrees."

"Jones." Tess's brows made a rapid climb. "You named him *Jones?*"

Jordan held up one hand, palm out. "Hey, don't look at me. He picked it himself."

Tess took a stab at making sense of that statement as she reached down and offered a hand for inspection. "Hello...Jones." The dog sniffed her fingers but shared no clues. Giving up, she gave the dog a hearty pat, then led her guests down the hall and introduced them to Sally.

"Glad to meet you and Jones, Jordan." Sally's smile grew to a grin as they shook hands. "It's so nice to know one's neighbors. My husband, Ben, and I live a couple of blocks down the street with our two boys."

"I recently moved in next door."

Looking up a considerable way at the man standing in front of her, Sally's brown eyes positively twinkled. "I know."

"Well, let's get you that cup of coffee," Tess said hastily, deciding it was time to break in. The last thing she wanted was for Jordan Trask to even suspect they'd been discussing him. Which they had, of course. At length.

While she retrieved another mug from a bleached-oak cabinet, her company seated themselves across from each other at the round glass table. The dog stretched out on the misty green tile near his master's feet.

Tess picked up the pot. "How do you like your coffee?"

"Just black." Jordan settled back in his chair and propped one booted foot on his knee.

"And how do you like Harmony?" Sally asked as a steaming mug was placed in front of him.

It was Jordan's turn to grin, and Tess's turn to fan herself. She felt the urge, at any rate. What the man could accomplish with a grin should be illegal, she thought, gazing down at him. It was positively deadly to the female half of the population.

"Harmony's terrific," he didn't hesitate to reply. "Strangers actually introduce themselves to you on the street, even in the busier downtown areas. It took a few times for me to expect it. Then again, one elderly, silver-haired lady didn't say a word when she picked out a cantaloupe for me at the grocery. She just walked up, shook a few, handed her choice over and left with a brisk nod."

"Probably Hester Goodbody," Sally concluded. "She tends to take charge, although in the nicest way. I think it's become second nature to her. Miss Hester taught a whole lot of us how to glue shiny stars on paper in the first grade. I think it was really a lesson in sitting still."

Jordan chuckled. "Well, whatever the case, she certainly was friendly."

"We're a friendly bunch, by and large. There are some confirmed grouches around, but not too many to ignore, if we chose to."

Abandoning her coffee, Sally leaned forward and propped her elbows on the table. She flicked a glance at Tess, now seated beside her, then returned her gaze to Jordan. "And speaking of friendliness," she said in an offhand tone, "I know we've only just met, but Ben and I are a having a backyard barbecue tonight if you'd like to stop by for some ribs and a beer. Most of the neighborhood will be there."

Tess froze with her mug halfway to her mouth, well aware that something was up. Not that she should be surprised, she told herself in the next breath, recalling the earlier twinkle in a pair of brown eyes. Sally wanted to get to know this man better—and she most especially wanted Tess to get to know him better. That was as clear as a neon sign in Las Vegas. At least it was to her. She could only hope it wasn't as blatantly plain to Jordan.

"Tess is coming," Sally added, oh-so-casually, placing her chin in the palm of one hand. If she caught the abruptly stern warning aimed from under her friend's lashes, she wasted no time in dismissing it and fluttering her own. "Maybe you two could come together."

And maybe I could strangle you, Tess thought, tightening her fingers around the mug handle.

The muscles in Jordan's throat worked as he took a long swallow of his coffee. Then he turned his head and looked directly at Tess.

"Maybe we could," he said. "I'd like to go. Would you go with me?"

"Oh, I'm sure she'd love to," Sally tossed in, as though the whole thing were happily settled.

And now it was past time to choke her, Tess reflected grimly. No jury made up of single women with well-meaning friends would convict her. They'd probably give her a medal. Before she could go about earning one, though, Sally pushed back her chair and all but leaped to her feet.

"My, how the time does fly! I have to get a move on. There's a mountain of potato salad to make and all sorts of things to do. See you tonight, Jordan. Don't bother walking me out, Tess." With that, she made a beeline for the doorway to the hall, sandal heels tapping the way, and turned to wave a merry goodbye.

Tess launched a steely, sidelong stare that silently said, *I'll get you for this.*

To which yet another lively twinkle in Sally's eye replied, *No, with any luck at all, you'll thank me.*

Chapter Three

Jordan resumed the task of finishing his coffee, aware that his question remained unanswered. Not that he'd been expecting to ask his gardening teacher to go anywhere with him that night. His sole intention, as he'd climbed her porch steps, was to see her again.

The truth was, he hadn't been able to convince himself to stay away any longer, not after keeping a sharp eye out for male visitors over the past several evenings and failing to see any calling on Tess Cameron. The field was clear, he'd presumed, an assumption just confirmed by her friend's obvious effort to throw them together. She would know far better than he if another man were in the picture.

Plainly, the answer was no.

On one hand, he was glad—probably more than he should be—that his neighbor was free to consider his suggestion. On the other, he couldn't help noting that she wasn't jumping at the chance to take him up on it.

Jordan glanced around a kitchen as homey as the one he currently called his own. Here, rainbow shades predominated and flowers ruled, covering the chair cushions and topping the windows. More flowers were strung out in a high border at the edge of the ceiling and a short glass vase holding an assortment of the real variety stood on the counter near the refrigerator.

And there, he noticed, a new and entirely different element had won out. Displayed on the front of the tall refrigerator, held up by a bright mix of small magnets, were several crayon drawings, all of trains.

"An artist in the family?" he asked with a nod at the pictures.

Tess's expression softened as a quick, fond smile appeared. "My daughter has her heart set on becoming a railroad engineer."

"Hmm. Interesting." Women did most everything these days, Jordan thought, including rocketing off into space. By the time eight-year-olds grew up, who knew what they'd be into?

"And I think she means business," Tess added, sounding like a proud mother. "One of the first words she learned to say was *choo-choo.* Ali was always more delighted with the toy train chugging around our Christmas tree than the ornaments on it."

Jordan waited, but she didn't go on. Finally he set his mug down with a soft clunk, deciding there was no use beating around the bush. "If you'd rather go alone tonight," he said, "I'll certainly understand."

Whatever he might have expected, it wasn't the reply he got.

"If *you'd* rather go alone, *I'll* be the one to understand," she said bluntly. "You were shanghaied into making that offer, and I intend to see that Sally gets what's coming to her."

One corner of his mouth kicked up at her abruptly dire tone. "What's the plan?"

"Boiling her in oil sounds great at the moment." Tess blew out a breath. "Or I could be downright cruel and break one of her fingernails. They're her pride and joy."

"That'll teach her." He stretched his long legs out in front of him and the dog at his feet yawned as if the movement had interrupted a nap. Thankfully, the cat was nowhere in sight. Jordan still wasn't sure that Jones had learned his lesson. Right now, he'd rather not put it to the test.

He had other things on his mind—mainly the answer he'd yet to get.

Reaching down, he brushed a hand over a furry head, then sat back and returned his gaze to the woman seated beside him. "Regardless of how it came about, I don't want to take back what I said earlier. Will you go with me?"

Another silent second passed before he finally got that reply. "All right, if you'd really like me to."

"I would," he said, and meant it.

Trouble was, he was beginning to think he liked it too much.

"THIS IS NO BIG DEAL," Tess reminded her reflection as she viewed it in a wide dresser mirror under the watchful light eyes of the cat stretched out in full glory on her cherry-wood queen-size bed. "It's not a real date, not even close. We just happen to be invited to the same party, so we're going together."

With that thought already firmly in mind when she'd dressed for the evening, she now wore what she'd planned to wear before Jordan Trask had arrived on the scene that morning. Her sleeveless white blouse edged with lace around a notched collar was comfortably suited to the warm weather, yet fancy enough for a casual party. Likewise her short coral-colored wraparound skirt and white mid-heeled sandals. Neighbors who had known her for years, even seen her grow up, would think she looked much the same as on a score of past occasions.

Which was as it should be, she reflected, because there was nothing all that exceptional about tonight. And if she repeated that to herself a dozen more times, maybe the swarm of butterflies flitting around in her stomach would calm down.

She could only hope.

Tess was still hoping, without great success, when the doorbell rang. "No big deal," she muttered under her breath as she headed down the stairs leading to the front entryway. Then she opened the door and the butterflies furiously flapped their way to new heights.

It was, she had to admit, a big, *big* deal.

Oh, not to the man who calmly gazed back at her, hazel eyes deepened to gleaming green by the jade polo shirt he wore with tan pants. Certainly not to him. But, for her, the bald truth was that this was a far-from-ordinary occasion—something, she decided, she would try mightily to keep as her secret.

To that end, she smiled a small smile and aimed for the lightest of tones. "You're right on time."

He returned her smile with his own crooked version. "All set to go?"

She nodded, switched on the porch light and pulled a house key from a side pocket of her skirt. "This is all I need."

Jordan watched as Tess secured the sturdy dead bolt on the door. That she had one at all surprised him a little. The house he'd rented sported only a standard lock on the knob and he hadn't given it another thought, not in a place like Harmony. The crime rate was probably close to zero. Hardened criminals could well be an endangered species here, a far cry from many of the places he'd known in the past.

But he didn't want to think about the past. That was behind him.

He'd rather consider the evening to come, although he realized it would hold some challenges. Keeping his eyes off Tess Cameron's legs was the first and foremost. It wouldn't do his temperature any good to start imagining how that creamy skin would feel under his palms. No damn good at all.

Jordan crossed his arms over his chest as they reached the bottom of the porch steps and started down a quiet street, side by side. He was her escort for the evening, he reminded himself, nothing more. He would take her to the party. He would see her home afterward. And he would try like blazes not to think about that dream.

No garden. No fragrant breezes. No welcoming woman waiting for him, wearing nothing but a—

"Tonight seems a little warmer than usual," Tess said.

Definitely warmer, he reflected with an inner grimace. "Maybe it will cool off later," he told her.

He could only hope.

THANKFULLY IT DID COOL OFF, the temperature dropping fairly rapidly once stars began to blink their way into the clear sky overhead.

And Jordan managed to cool off, as well.

Then again, he hadn't had much time during the past hour to look at Tess's legs, he had to admit. Ever since Ben Mendoza, a raven-haired, dark-eyed, big-boned man with a smile as wide as his native Texas, had pressed a cold beer bottle into Jordan's hand and hauled him away for a lively game of horseshoes, the woman he'd escorted had only been glimpsed in the chatty crowd milling around the spacious backyard.

Now he had another beer in one hand and a pair of long steel tongs in the other, turning ribs on one of four sizzling charcoal grills set at one side of the yard near a high stone fence and trying to look like he'd been doing it all his life. Probably no male in the history of mankind, starting with the first caveman to roast a leg of something over an open fire, had ever confessed to having less than total skill in the outdoor-cooking department. Jordan didn't plan on being the first.

"Having a good time?" his hostess, all decked out in something pink and gauzy, asked as she walked up and inspected his efforts.

"Yes," he said, and it wasn't just to be polite. The whole flock of Harmony residents present this evening, from the youngest to the oldest and every stage in between, were clearly enjoying themselves. And so was he. How amazed would they be, he wondered, if he told them he'd never attended a friendly neighbor's party before this very night?

Rowdy parties, yes. Plenty of them in his younger, wilder days. But none like this one.

Sally took a hefty whiff of the spicy aroma rising from the grill. "Smells great. You must be an expert."

One corner of his mouth slid upward. "Could be."

"Sorry I had to rush away this morning." Brown

eyes sparkled as they met his. "I'm glad you and Tess decided to come together."

The other edge of his mouth rose in the same slow slide. "I figured you would be."

A fleeting smile surfaced. "Ah, yes. I won't pretend I didn't meddle. I did. But I only meant to help. Sometimes these things need a little nudge. Trouble is, I think Tess would like to nudge me flat off my feet and on my rear." Sally aimed a wary glance around her. "Uh-oh. Here she comes. Gotta go. I've managed to keep two steps ahead of her since she arrived packing a razor-sharp gleam in her eye." With that, Sally whipped around and fled.

The gleam was there, all right. It had been trained on him just a week earlier, so he had no trouble recognizing it as Tess approached. She halted beside him, eyes narrowed and fixed on her friend's retreating back.

"She can run, but she can't hide. Not forever." Tess blew out a breath. "I'm getting some good exercise, at any rate. Along with an appetite. When will the ribs be done?"

"Soon," he replied, figuring that was a safe enough guess.

As she looked his way, her gaze took on another gleam, this one of amusement. "I like the outfit."

He dropped a glance at the black cotton apron his host had urged on him, its bib top sporting flaming red letters that declared *Real Men Do Their Smoking On The Grill.* "It's a fashion statement, all right."

The wry remark won him a quiet chuckle. "How did you wind up cooking?"

He shrugged. "Beats me. It just sort of happened."

She nodded wisely. ''Ben wanted to make you feel comfortable, so he put you to work. Are you?''

He cocked a brow. ''Working?''

''Comfortable.''

He wasn't, not entirely. Seeing how her fine-textured skin glowed under the flickering light of a tall metal torch staked nearby had his mind bent on wandering to forbidden places. And it would take some effort to keep it in check. But he could hardly say anything of the sort.

''Comfortable enough,'' he replied, and firmly returned his gaze to the task at hand. ''My stomach could use some food, though. Once these ribs are ready, I plan on doing them justice.''

THEY BOTH DID their dinner justice as they sat at one end of a long pine picnic table, sharing it with several other people. Jordan had chosen to sit opposite Tess rather than beside her, and as the meal progressed, he gave silent thanks for his foresight. He didn't need their thighs touching, that was for sure, no matter how briefly or casually. Just watching the woman across from him lick sauce off her lips with a delicate pink tongue had his wayward thoughts considering the private merits of being licked himself...and not by a dog.

What he did need, he decided as he finished the last of his ribs, was a distraction.

''How about some music?'' one of the men at the table asked, raising his voice over the low buzz of conversation.

''Yeah, Floyd,'' another chimed in. ''When you and the boys are done stuffing yourselves, let's hear a few tunes.''

That suited Jordan to a tee. Whatever he might have imagined would follow, though, it wasn't an impromptu performance by a barbershop quartet. Yet that's what he found himself listening to minutes later, when three men with varying amounts of graying hair gathered to stand shoulder-to-shoulder behind a much younger man of about twenty seated in a wheelchair.

Jordan clapped along with the rest of the crowd at the end of "Down By The Old Millstream." "They're good," he told Tess, leaning in her direction over the table. "Where did they come up with the idea to get together?"

"In a barbershop." She smiled at his suddenly blank look. "And that's the truth. Floyd Crenshaw, the tall man in the middle, owns the only genuine, old-time barbershop left in the downtown area. The two men standing beside him are longtime customers. My dad used to be the fourth member of the group. Now Brady, Floyd's youngest son, has taken over."

"He won the horseshoe toss." Jordan studied the sandy-haired young man, who seemed fit enough, despite the disability. Probably not illness-related, he decided. An accident of some kind, most likely. It was a damn shame, but there it was. "The guy's got an arm made for throwing, and a deadly aim."

"Brady's tough to beat," Tess agreed as the opening strains of "Lida Rose" began. "He's competitive. Even more so, I'd say, than before the wheelchair entered the scene three years ago. And he's a darn good singer. My dad's baritone was hardly missed, though no one would wound his ego by telling him so."

The song ended in another lively round of applause

moments later, and once again Jordan leaned toward his companion. "What did your father do here before he moved?" he asked, both to further the conversation and because he was curious about how people earned a living. As pleasant as Harmony was, there was no major industry in the immediate area to produce jobs.

"He worked for Arizona Electric for years," Tess said, "first as a lineman, then as foreman of a large crew. Now, from what I've been hearing lately, he's mixing the joys of part-time work as an ace electrician with the hardships of watching television while sprawled in a recliner."

The last came out so dryly Jordan's mouth curved. "What about your mother?"

"She was, and is, a full-time homemaker."

Jordan nodded. "I don't suppose homemakers get to slow down much."

"Probably not as much as they're entitled to in most cases," Tess agreed. "Still, I was pleased when my folks decided to move to San Diego. My mom wanted to give life by the ocean a try, and I'm glad she got her way. She deserved it." Tess propped her elbows on the table. "The house I'm living in now was theirs. I sold a smaller place not too far from here and took over their mortgage. Which made my folks happy, because I'm their only child, and they loved the house and wanted it to stay in the family." She paused for a beat. "How about your family?"

He shrugged. "I don't have a lot. Only an older brother I haven't seen in years."

A frown formed, sobering her expression. "Your parents are gone?"

"Yeah." And it would have been nice to say he

truly missed them. But he didn't, Jordan had to admit. Somehow he doubted they'd ever wanted to be parents. Certainly they'd never gone out of their way to show affection to their children. His brother had packed up and left the Trask homestead—a drab apartment in a dust-clogged town on a flat stretch of southern Nevada—as soon as he could manage it, and Jordan couldn't blame him. He'd done exactly the same when he'd got his chance.

Another tune started up at that point, and Jordan again welcomed the distraction. Dwelling on his family had never been one of his favorite pastimes. He returned his gaze to the performers, already having noted a change in the music even before he saw that Brady Crenshaw now strummed an acoustic guitar to blend in with the smooth vocals, while a second young man—another Crenshaw by the look of him—tapped a rhythmic beat on a set of bongo drums.

The song was an old Sinatra standard, a bluesy ballad, and several people apparently judged it danceable enough to stand up to give it a try, including the host and hostess, who had been seated clear across the yard.

"If Fast-Foot Sally glides by anywhere near me, she's mine," Tess declared with grim intent.

"If your friend is smart," Jordan muttered under his breath, "she'll stay well out of reach."

The woman in question seemed to heed that advice as she and her husband drifted closer and came to a halt on Jordan's side of the table. They separated, smiling at each other. And then Sally was pulling Jordan to his feet. With the element of surprise in her favor, she managed it with little trouble. They were headed toward the middle of the makeshift dance floor in the center of the grassy yard before he could issue a protest.

"I'm not much good at this," he said, which was no less than the truth. He enjoyed listening to music. Moving to it had never been his strong suit.

"It's a slow one," his hostess pointed out. "Practicing will only make you better."

Jordan gave in to his fate with the thinnest of sighs, placed an arm lightly around his partner's waist and began to move, shuffling his feet.

She grinned up at him. "There, you see. You're doing fine."

"If I stomp on your toes, don't say I didn't warn you." Gazing over her head, he saw that Tess and Ben had joined the dancers. It gave him some satisfaction to note that the big Texan wasn't demonstrating any fancier moves than he was. At least he had that small comfort, he thought.

But not for long.

Midway through the second chorus, Ben closed the gap between them and executed a quick spin. Legs braced to halt his own momentum, he launched his partner straight at Jordan and Sally, then reached for the hand his wife suddenly freed to extend his way, and tugged her toward him in the next breath. Tess landed in the vacant spot an instant later, completing a swift switch of partners worthy of a Broadway musical production.

Jordan couldn't help but admire it, even though the outcome left him holding a somewhat breathless and thoroughly disgruntled woman. "Sally put him up to it," she grumbled, hauling in air. "I know it. And after that little performance, it'll look ridiculous if we don't continue dancing."

"So we will." Jordan resumed his slow shuffle. "It won't be hard to keep up with me," he told her dryly.

Keep up? With *him?* Tess drew in more air as realization dawned. All at once every inch of her zinged to full awareness of just how close they were at that very moment. Almost chest-to-chest close.

Or, rather, chest to breast.

Somehow her feet kept moving and her lungs kept working. Somehow her gaze remained steady as she aimed it beyond a broad shoulder and looked up at a moonlit sky. Basic instincts had assumed control. Which was a good thing, because most of her brain seemed to be on hold.

She might tell herself it was silly, that she'd shared many a dance with numerous men in the past, and they hadn't all been longtime friends and neighbors. Parties during her early college days in the Phoenix area had produced a variety of young and attractive partners, and she'd kicked up her high heels on more than one occasion.

But she had to admit that she'd never encountered anyone quite like the man who held her now, never been so physically reminded of the fact that she was female. Not even marriage and motherhood had prepared her for her body's total and undeniable response. From the top of her head to the tips of her toes, Jordan Trask made her truly feel like a woman.

"Sorry I'm not more of a dancer," he said, his voice a rough whisper at her ear. "You'll probably be glad when this song is over."

No, she wouldn't. How could she, given the wonders that came with being in this man's arms? "Not especially," she murmured. "I've always liked this song."

She pulled back slightly to gaze up at him and awareness soared to new heights. They were surrounded by people, yet it seemed as if, for this singular moment in time, no one existed but the two of them. It had to be her imagination, she told herself. He couldn't be feeling what she was feeling.

Could he?

The last notes of the music died away at that point. The song was over. And Tess decided then and there to go home—before she started imagining who knew what.

"Thanks for the dance," she said with deliberate mildness.

"Thanks for putting up with my shuffling." He released her and took a step back. "Can I get you another glass of wine?"

With a swift shake of her head, she said, "It's getting late. I have to go."

He didn't point out that it was barely ten o'clock. He just said, "I'll walk you home."

She brushed a stray lock of hair back from her face. "You don't have to, you know. You could stay and enjoy yourself."

It was his turn to shake his head. "I'm ready to go, too, but first I suppose we should say goodbye to our hosts."

Tess aimed a look around her. "Somehow it doesn't amaze me that they're nowhere in sight. I'll talk to Sally tomorrow."

"Okay," Jordan agreed as they started for the front of the house. "Will you tell her I said thanks for inviting me?"

"I'd be glad to. Right after I tell her a few other things."

THEY WERE HALFWAY HOME by the time Jordan finally decided that, with the least encouragement on her part, he would kiss the woman walking beside him when they got to her door. It was something he'd been mulling over ever since he'd released her after that dance and dropped his arms when he only wanted to haul her closer, because holding her had felt so damn good. But he'd figured she wouldn't appreciate being swept up in full view of a crowd of onlookers and carried off into the night. Which was exactly what everything inside him had firmly urged him to do, right then and there.

No, he'd settle for a kiss. And not a long one, either. Just a short, small taste of those naturally rosy lips. That's what he had in mind.

Jordan snorted under his breath. Who was he kidding? His mind had little to do with it. Other parts of him were a lot more involved. They were, in fact, primed for action. But he could—and would—keep them in check.

The question was: Would he get any encouragement?

Tess hadn't said much beyond a few words since they'd left the party. Neither had he. Still there was no uneasiness in the silence between them, not that he could detect. Could be she was comfortable being alone with him despite that humming instant of up-close-and-personal eye contact during their dance. Or she might be too busy plotting revenge for her friend's meddling to spare a thought for discomfort.

Whatever the case, he figured it was to his advantage. If she wasn't uptight about the situation, chances were a brief good-night kiss could be taken as no more than a casual end to a pleasant evening. She didn't have to know how much he wanted a taste of her.

Just a small taste, Jordan reminded himself, and repeated the inner warning for good measure when they arrived at their destination minutes later and mounted the low front steps. As they stood under the soft glow cast by the porch light overhead, her fine-grained skin again took on a golden gleam, and Jordan's hands fisted in his pockets, where they'd remained during the short walk.

He vowed to keep them there and off that petal-smooth skin. No matter what.

"Thanks for seeing me home," Tess said, finally breaking the quiet all around them.

"You're welcome," he replied, stark huskiness in his tone.

She drew a sharp breath, as if she'd recognized what his vocal chords had revealed. It was something a man had a difficult time hiding when a female was in sight who stirred everything male in him. He'd been lucky to conceal it this long.

Once again their gazes locked. Once again silence stretched between them. But this time there was nothing comfortable about it.

This time, tension snapped in the calm, balmy air.

"Well, I suppose I should go in," Tess murmured at last. But she didn't move a muscle, just stared at him with clear blue eyes. And that turned out to be all the encouragement Jordan required.

Without a word, he bent his head and put his mouth on hers, felt soft lips part slightly under his, and didn't think it was in shock. In welcome, was what he told himself, what he wanted to believe as he tilted his chin and angled his mouth for a better fit. His tongue probed gently, gradually found entry, and tasted what awaited him.

Just one small taste.

And all at once his whole body clenched with need and craved more. A lot more. So much more, the sudden hunger twisting through him threatened to make him growl. He needed more badly, and he needed it *now*.

He didn't realize his hands had left his pockets until his palms cupped delicate shoulders, had no awareness of his arms tugging a slender figure closer until soft breasts brushed the solid wall of his chest. The kiss, already longer than he'd bargained for, turned hard and heated in a hurry as the puzzling pull he'd experienced on their first meeting made a swift return. Far stronger now, it drew him in, urged him on and wiped out any thought of bringing things to a halt.

The hell with everything, he told himself. He wasn't stopping. Not yet.

Tess clutched the corded forearms of the man who held her and tried to cling as tightly to her common sense. They were in clear view of the entire neighborhood, kissing each other as if their lives depended on it, as though the world would end if they so much as paused from a greedy meld of lips, teeth and tongues to take the barest breath.

Thank goodness most of her neighbors were still at the party, because she was participating to the hilt in what seemed like total madness, she couldn't deny. Jordan might have initially taken her by surprise, but she'd caught up quickly. Three years was a long time to go without kissing a virile male. She hadn't realized exactly how long until a firm mouth had come down on hers.

Yet the bald truth was that more than mere years separated her from the heady wonders of being kissed like this, with such towering need and single-minded intensity. She had, in fact, never been kissed like this. Ever. Never had she felt as if reality were about to go up in smoke. When it did in the next instant, Tess clung even tighter to those strong arms and gave herself up to the moment.

No past existed; no future waited. Only the present mattered, and pulling her mind back to full awareness of her surroundings was no longer an option. She'd already made the choice to lose herself in the pleasure this man's kiss could give her. And to enjoy every minute of it.

Jordan was the one who eventually pulled back, halting the kiss as abruptly as it had begun. For a long moment he stared down at Tess, a stunned look in his eyes, as if he couldn't quite believe what had just happened. Then he took a deep breath and found his voice.

"I'm sorry," he told her. "I think that, uh, got a bit out of hand."

A bit out of hand?

That was, Tess reflected as she pulled in air, like saying an earthquake right off the Richter scale was a bit of a jolt. And as far as her muddled brain could recall, the ground had rocked only seconds ago.

"I think it did," she managed to say. "Get out of hand, that is. But, ah, no harm done." Her heart was still beating, at any rate. Goodness, was it ever! She released her death grip on Jordan and backed up a quick step.

"I—" He cleared his throat. "I guess I should be going, but I'll wait until you get in."

Rather than making a second effort to speak, she merely nodded, retrieved the house key from a pocket of her skirt and unlocked the door, grateful her hand was steady enough to accomplish it. Stepping inside, she switched on the hall light.

"Tess..."

She turned around, made herself look straight at the man who'd kissed her witless and found his gaze trained on her.

"Would you like to go to dinner tomorrow night?" he asked, his voice still husky enough to send a shiver down her spine.

What she'd like was another kiss. And not tomorrow night. But if those firm lips repeated that torrid tangle with hers, she might very well spontaneously combust and burn the house down. The cat, she thought fleetingly, would never forgive her.

Tess groped for the mildest tone she could muster, which wasn't exactly calm, cool and collected. "Dinner sounds fine."

His gaze didn't waver. "I'll pick you up around six."

"Okay." She shut the door as he turned away and started down the steps. Then she sank back against it and let out a long breath. She'd learned something in the past few minutes, something she was still having trouble believing, although it was true. It simply had to be. There was no way she could have mistaken what had just happened, or what it meant. No way she could come to any conclusion, but the one she'd reached. No way she could stop the blood from rushing through her veins as four words repeated in her mind.

Jordan Trask wants me.

It seemed that larger-than-life men did involve themselves with down-to-earth women, at least occasionally. Maybe, she told herself with the beginnings of a shaky smile, she'd be taking a lover soon. After that kiss, she had to admit she was ready.

More than ready.

JORDAN WASN'T SMILING a little later that same evening. He was, in fact, scowling at his reflection in the bathroom mirror. He had taken what he figured could well be the longest and coldest shower in the history of indoor plumbing.

And he was still on slow burn.

He reached down and hitched a blue towel more firmly around his waist. What the hell had he been thinking of to lose control that way? And with someone like Tess, of all people? Sure, she was no innocent. She was a mother, after all.

But she was still...*wholesome.* It was the only word he could come up with. She wasn't a woman to take a lover at the drop of a hat, that was for sure. Not hardly.

If he was going to get involved with her, he'd have to take it slow and easy. And he'd be getting involved, he knew, even though he'd been telling himself only days earlier that the last thing he needed was a woman in his life.

Now he knew exactly what he needed. And badly.

"But you have to watch your step, Trask," he told himself as he opened the bathroom door and started down the hall. "You could screw everything up if you come on too strong too fast."

Jones greeted his owner at the bedroom door with a swift wag of a thin tail.

"You don't know how simple your life is," he told the dog as he tossed the towel aside, got in bed and pulled the top sheet over him.

Jones sat on the rug at Jordan's side and cocked a furry head, as though considering that statement.

"Yeah, pal, you've got it made," Jordan muttered, lifting a hand to shove strands of damp hair back from his forehead. "You eat, you sleep, you do your duty out in the backyard when nature calls and I get to clean up after you." He heaved a long sigh. "You don't have any idea what it's like to have real problems—not the downright damnedest kind a female can provide, at any rate."

The dog growled softly in response, as if to take exception to that comment.

Jordan fixed his companion with a probing look, reminding himself that he was far from sure of his new pet's history. "Known a few, have you?" he ventured, and had to snort out a laugh when the dog seemed to roll dark eyes. "Okay, maybe you have, but it gets even more complicated when the female in question happens to be human, trust me."

He leaned back against a plump pillow and stared up at the ceiling, thinking that he'd better come up with a plan to handle his current problem, and quick. Asking Tess out on a date was a good start, he had to admit, especially since she hadn't turned him down flat despite how he'd been ready to gobble her up whole less than an hour ago. At least he was getting another chance to show her he wasn't a slave to his libido. He could—and would—hold himself in check.

In fact, from now on he'd jam his hands into his pockets every time he got the barest itch to touch, he vowed, and keep them there come hell or high water, because as much as he wanted and needed Tess Cameron in his bed, he was dead certain of one thing.

She wasn't ready.

Chapter Four

"So you've come to that conclusion, have you?" Tess folded her arms under her breasts and tapped a canvas-shod foot on the beige linoleum floor of the landscaping service's front sales area, one of the few places in the store sporting some fairly open space. Various members of the plant world, from tall and lean to short and squat, occupied much of the rest of the large warehouse-style building, with more spilling out into a walled courtyard at the rear. "At least you're finally looking me in the eye," she added, raising a brow.

"I decided it had to be safer to see you at work," Sally admitted as they faced each other in muted sunshine slanting through the thick glass ceiling overhead. "That way, maybe someone will come to my rescue if you're still bent on revenge." Sally's gently pointed chin went up a notch. "And I'm standing by my statement, no matter what. I *do* think you and Jordan are a good match, and I'm not at all sorry I threw you two together. Are *you?*"

Tess was a long way from sure how to answer that question. At least if she and a certain man weren't dating, she thought, she undoubtedly wouldn't be feeling as frustrated as she was today. Then again, she didn't regret those dates—just how they had all ended so far. "I guess not," she said at last.

"Does that mean you've decided not to take me apart for my good intentions?" A small smile appeared, brightening Sally's expression. "I can go to Florida in one piece?"

Tess thought about that for a minute and finally nodded. "Chasing two healthy kids all over Disney World for a few days while your loving husband takes the easy way out and heads off to investigate Orlando's golf courses will probably be enough to even the score."

"God, you could be right." Sally sighed. "Before the whole thing starts with a trip to the airport at the crack of dawn tomorrow, do I at least get a hint as to how things are going between you and Jordan?"

Tess dropped her arms and brushed a hand down the front of her khaki work pants. "We've been out on a few dinner dates."

"No, really?" Sally replied with a roll of her eyes. "Come on, Tess, half the people in town probably know that much, right down to which restaurants got your business and what you both wore on each occasion. Not to mention what you ordered, how much you ate, and so on and so forth. This is one of your best chums talking, remember? I'm after the juicy stuff."

"Hmm. Well, there's not a great deal to pass along when it comes to the juicier side of things." Tess turned and started toward one side of the room, where a large carton rested on a long, slatted pine table. "If you want to continue this discussion, it'll have to be while I unload this shipment of flowerpots we just got in from Mexico.''

Sally came up behind her. ''That's very attractive,'' she said, offering the compliment as Tess pulled a shiny, glazed clay pot delicately edged with small squares of deep blue tile from the carton.

''Should be a good seller.'' Tess set the pot on the table and reached in for another one.

''Spoken like a true businesswoman.'' Sally pushed up the sleeves of the red-and-white striped blouse she wore with white slacks. ''I'll help unload, since I'm such a good pal. Plus I'm not ready to let the fascinating subject of you and your hunky neighbor drop.''

''Figures.'' Tess blew out a breath. ''Wish I had something fascinating to report.''

Sally dug into the carton. ''Don't tell me the man is boring in any way, shape or form. I absolutely refuse to believe it.''

''No, he's hardly that. He's just...careful.''

That made Sally blink. ''Careful? As in cautious?''

''Uh-huh. It's plain he likes to take things slow.'' Tess paused for a beat. ''Very slow.''

Sally set down the pot she'd pulled out, this one trimmed in gleaming turquoise. ''Does that mean he hasn't so much as kissed you yet?'' Brown eyes were frankly incredulous.

''No. But then there are kisses and, ah, kisses.''

The first they'd shared, Tess thought, had rocked her to the core and nearly off her feet. Just the memory threatened to have her toes tingling. Every one that had followed, unfortunately, had been no more than the average good-night, I-had-a-good-time variety. A warm brush of lips, but little else. And always with Jordan's hands shoved firmly into his pockets.

Frustration was taking on a whole new meaning, she had to admit. How long would it be, she'd been asking herself for days, before she felt those hands on her?

"If you're implying that Jordan Trask doesn't know what to do with his mouth, Tess, I'm headed toward flat-out disbelief again. I would have bet the farm that the man's lips—not to mention his tongue—" Sally slid in, wiggling a brow "—were well up to speed."

"I wouldn't put it down to lack of knowledge," Tess had to concede. "Let's just say that he seems to be, um, restraining himself." *Way too much.*

It wasn't that he was incapable of passion, she knew. He was more than capable in that particular department. Which, as far as she was concerned, only made the whole thing harder to understand.

Sally's sudden smile was wide and definitely wicked around the edges. "Maybe he needs another nudge in the right direction. This time from you. Gentlemanly restraint can't be that difficult to overcome, not if that's all it is. Have you thought about—how should I put this—*seducing* him?"

Tess laughed in spite of herself. She'd never seduced a man in her life. Not even close. "I'm hardly femme fatale material, Sal."

Her friend dismissed that statement with an airy wave of one hand. "Every woman has a bit of femme fatale lurking inside her, I'd say. We just have to let it loose."

"Sure we do," Tess said dryly. "I'm barely able to keep mine under control."

Sally dug in for another pot and grunted with the effort to pull one from the bottom of the carton. "You can joke about it if you want to, but— Oh, no! I tore a nail!"

Tess had to bite her lip to foil another laugh, this one of pure amusement, as the woman beside her yanked a hand out of the carton, as if a wild beast had just showed its teeth and tried to take a nibble. Sally took a step back and studied her middle finger in dismay. "Good grief. I have to patch it right away before the thing splits off entirely. I can't start my vacation with a stub for a nail, for heaven's sake."

"With luck, it'll survive the crisis," Tess assured her friend solemnly, tongue fully in cheek.

But Sally, clearly beyond teasing, was already headed for the open double doors to the parking lot. "I'll send you a postcard from Florida," she called over her shoulder. "That is if I can get my hyper kids to stand still long enough to let me buy one."

"Great," Tess said, with the beginnings of a wry grin that faded in a flash as she caught sight of someone standing at one side of the doorway. As usual, he looked devastating in a casual knit shirt paired with faded Levi's. As usual, everything in her comfortable, ordinary world paled in contrast to the far-from-ordinary image he presented. And, as was annoyingly usual these days, she found herself wanting more. A lot more than he seemed willing to give, for some reason.

Blast it. What was wrong with the man?

For his part, Jordan's gaze settled on the woman walking toward him with quick steps. "Something wrong?" he asked, well aware that Sally Mendoza didn't look happy.

"My nail got broken," she told him, holding up one hand to show a string of scarlet-tipped fingers.

"That's too bad," Jordan murmured, asking himself what else he could say under the circumstances. It wasn't exactly a 911 situation. Then again, he hadn't lived as long as he had without discovering that things were sometimes viewed differently by the female half of the population. It was what made them so damned intriguing.

Sally squared her shoulders bravely. "It will be all right, I'm sure. I just have to get home and take care of it."

"Well, ah, good luck."

"Thanks. By the way," Sally added in an undertone as she started to slip around him, "if you're open to some advice, it's not always wise, I think, to be too careful."

Jordan's brows drew together in a flash. He was intrigued, all right, not to mention mystified. "I beg your pardon?"

"Take my word for it," his one-time hostess said as she kept on moving, "sometimes you just have to let yourself go and throw caution to the wind."

"And what's that supposed to mean?" he wondered out loud, and also to himself, as it turned out, because Sally was now several steps past him and didn't spare a backward glance as she continued on her way.

Still puzzled, Jordan switched his gaze ahead and found another woman studying him. As usual, even dressed in strictly practical work clothes and wearing little makeup, she looked good enough for a hungry man to gobble up whole. As usual, he was in grave danger of getting lost in those clear blue eyes. And, as was becoming increasingly usual these days, he shoved his hands into his pockets before they could reach for her.

Look but don't touch.

He'd made that his motto on their first official date, and he had stuck to it ever since. It had not been easy. In fact, it was getting harder by the minute. He would continue to stick to it, though, he told himself as he started forward with firm steps, because he had to give Tess Cameron all the time she needed to get comfortable with him. However much he might want her, he wouldn't risk losing her again by coming on too strong too soon.

''Hi,'' he said when he stood a few feet away. ''If your thirst for revenge did your friend's nail in, I'll have to mark you as a dangerous woman.''

The corners of Tess's mouth curved softly. ''Sally managed to do it herself, but I can't say I was exactly heartbroken.'' She lifted a hand and brushed a stray honey-brown curl back from her face. ''I didn't expect to see you today.''

He hadn't expected it, either, not until he'd left a coffee shop nearby after a soup and sandwich lunch and discovered he couldn't resist the urge to get at least a glimpse of her before their date tomorrow night. ''I was in the area, so I thought I'd stop by and take a look at where you work,'' he said in the most casual of tones.

She accepted his comment with a nod. ''You picked the right day, as it turns out. I normally spend Monday through Thursday doing whatever outside jobs crop up, provided the weather cooperates, and Friday here helping with the retail part of the business.''

Jordan glanced around him. "Can't say I've ever been in a landscaping place before."

Green was the operative word here, he decided. He'd never seen so many shades of it grouped together so closely and couldn't put an exact name now to most of what he viewed. They were merely trees, bushes and plants to him, because he didn't know any more about greenery than he did about flowers. Luckily Tess no longer expected any expertise in that field.

She knew that much about him, at any rate. Knew his food preferences, too, since the subject had naturally come up over the meals they'd shared. Good, simple fare and plenty of it was what he liked best. Thankfully the restaurant owners in Harmony seemed to agree, as did the woman he'd been escorting. He would have taken her to the fanciest of French restaurants if she'd expressed a desire to go and one could be found in the vicinity. But she'd turned out to be a bigger fan of basic dishes than fancy sauces, which suited him just fine.

Not that food had been the only topic to surface during the time they'd spent together, Jordan reflected. For the most part, conversation had flowed easily as they'd talked about many things—talked about pretty much everything, in fact, except anything to do with the private details of his life before he'd come here.

He had deliberately avoided that particular topic, concentrating on the present as much as possible, and didn't plan on changing that situation. As far as he was concerned, few of his personal memories were worth a mention. They were no longer important, not to him.

As if to prove the case to be just the opposite with

her, Tess said, "I can remember coming to Zieglers as a wide-eyed kid with a healthy imagination and pretending that I was in the middle of a jungle."

"And I caught you swinging more than once from one of my little trees," a gruff voice added. "Got it into your brain that you were a monkey, most likely."

The man who approached had to be close to seventy, though his long spine was still ramrod straight and his walk was still spry. Thinning gray hair rimmed a head held proudly high. Even dressed in the same khaki-colored uniform Tess wore, with the name of the landscaping service stitched on a front shirt pocket in bold green letters, he had a quiet air of unquestionable command about him. Used to running his own show, Jordan thought.

Tess chuckled. "I may have been a monkey, Hank, but I was smart enough to get on your good side. I never left here without a small cutting you'd snip off for me."

"Wanted you to have your own plants to fuss over so you wouldn't bother mine," the man grumbled, even as a warm glint in shrewd eyes the shade of light smoke belied his griping.

Tess went on to introduce her new neighbor. "Jordan was just telling me that he's never been in a place like this," she said as a firm handshake was completed.

"Well then, I'd be glad to give you a quick tour," Hank offered easily.

But Jordan didn't miss how the glint in smoky eyes had abruptly turned probing and now held more than a hint of steel. It all but said, *If you're planning on being more than a neighbor, you'd better treat this woman right.*

He met the other man's gaze head-on as they took each other's measure, held it as he issued both spoken and silent words. "I'd appreciate whatever time you can spare." *And I got your message, loud and clear.*

Hank nodded slowly, and something in the gesture made Jordan think he'd passed at least an initial test. "Come on, son," Hank told him. "We'll start by introducing you to a lady brave enough to take a chance on me over forty years ago, back when I was a guy who only wanted to grow things and didn't have two nickels to rub together."

"For which stroke of good fortune you should still be thanking your lucky stars," Tess tacked on. Then she waved them away. "I'll catch up with you after I finish unloading these flowerpots."

Jordan flashed her a grin. "Be careful not to break any fingernails."

AS THE TOUR CONTINUED, Jordan met Violet Ziegler, a sturdily built woman with a crown of well-groomed hair caught up high in a neat bun that shone like burnished pewter. Tawny eyes gleaming, she stood guard over the cash register and took his measure much as her husband had before offering a courteous smile. "So you're the young man Tess has been seeing."

That statement hardly surprised Jordan, not at this point. Even if Tess hadn't so much as mentioned their budding relationship to anyone, after a few weeks in his new environment he was conscious the odds were that many of Harmony's residents knew about it.

"Yes, ma'am, I am," he said.

"Now that you've had a chance to settle in, what do you think of our city?" Violet asked, arching a thin silver brow.

Jordan considered the meal he'd just finished. As a single man, he was used to eating alone more often than not, but so many people had stopped by his booth to offer a short greeting that he'd been a long way from lonely in that coffee shop. Somehow, he'd felt a part of the group, even though many of the names of his fellow diners remained unknown to him. That was simply the kind of place Harmony was.

"I think it could be as close to perfection as I'll ever get," he replied, fully meaning every word.

Violet's expression abruptly sobered, but before Jordan could even begin to wonder what might have prompted that, her smile was back. "It's not perfect, no. But it is a good place to live. I hope you enjoy your time here." She glanced at her husband, and now her smile turned fond. "Take good care of our visitor, Hank."

His host did exactly that, keeping the conversation going as they moved toward the back of the store and out into the rear courtyard. In the process, it didn't take him long to figure out that his guest was less than an expert gardener. Jordan knew that for a fact by the way Hank's tone took a subtle slide into instructor mode as he pointed out the various types of plants they passed. Some of them sounded familiar, others were a complete mystery. All in all, it wasn't a bad way to spend an afternoon, he decided. Especially since he could see Tess in the process.

She hadn't invaded his dreams recently, but she was turning up in his waking thoughts on a regular basis. Even if he had put some effort into changing that fact, he was far from certain he could have blocked her out. Somehow, some way, she'd gotten under his skin. Maybe it was that first kiss. And maybe tomorrow night, Jordan mused, he'd take a chance and kiss her a little deeper, a little harder, a little longer.

But he was still keeping his hands off her.

"Don't know what I'm going to do about this one," Hank muttered as he came to a halt in front of the arched doorway leading back into the store.

Jordan glanced down, following the other man's gaze to the side of the door, and found his eyes landing on a small plant growing in a large terra-cotta pot set on the concrete floor. The term *growing* might be a stretch, he had to admit. Even to his inexperienced eyes, *struggling to survive* seemed a lot more accurate. The plant's scrawny center, circled by thin branches with a sketchy covering of leaves, looked frail enough to fold under its own weight, and probably would have if it hadn't been tied to a short wooden stake.

"What is it?" he asked, looking up at his host.

"A tomato plant." With his head still bent, Hank shook it sadly. "At least that's what nature had in mind for it, though I doubt it will ever produce a crop. Lord knows, I've done everything I can think of to help it shape up, and that's considerable, trust me. I hate to say so, but it looks as if I'll have to concede defeat on this one. Which is close to a first for me, I can tell you."

Jordan frowned. "What will happen to it?"

Hank shrugged a bony shoulder. "Can't see a customer taking it, even a gardening buff who wants a real challenge, which this surely would be. Probably best to give the poor thing a decent burial in the compost pile."

A decent burial. The phrase rang in Jordan's mind

even as those scarce, scraggly leaves seemed to wilt right under his gaze. As strange as it might sound if he were to attempt to explain it, he could almost see hope draining away. And what would be left? A decent burial...

He didn't think about what he said next. The words just came out, soft yet firm. "I'd like to buy it."

Tess walked up just in time to hear Jordan's declaration. Which described it exactly, she told herself. There'd been nothing tentative about his statement—or the sudden resolute clench of his jaw.

"Given the shape it's in, I believe that'd be a mistake, son," Hank told him.

"I don't," Jordan countered quietly, still staring at the plant. "I think it can be salvaged."

Hank's weathered forehead furrowed at that last remark. "What makes you say so?"

"Damned if I know," Jordan muttered in response. At that moment, it seemed to Tess as if he were talking as much to himself as to his companions. "I just figure I have to give it a try."

Hank made another attempt to discourage his visitor, citing his admitted inexperience, and Tess found herself chiming in, chiefly because she had more than a hunch from the set cast of Jordan's features that he would take it hard if the plant didn't make it. And she was sure it wouldn't. Not after Hank, with his long years in the business and green grower's thumb, had failed to make it thrive.

Violet didn't say much when she nipped over for a minute between customers to see what the fuss was about. She merely issued a gentle sigh and shook her head as she gazed down at the object in question—and that basically said it all.

Jordan stuck to his guns as the discussion ranged back and forth until Hank was the one to sigh heavily. "Okay, I'll sell you the pot, but I can't in good conscience take any money for the plant. I can let you have a pamphlet that will spell out directions on watering and fertilizing, and Tess can pick out the best spot in your yard to allow for the right amount of sun. But that's about all we can do." He lifted a hand and ran it through his hair. "The rest, son, is between you and Mother Nature."

Jordan dipped his head in a brisk nod. "I guess it is."

He was being stubborn to the core, Tess thought. And she could only admire him for it. This hardheaded male wasn't hesitating to buck the odds, no matter how futile the whole thing might be. He wasn't reluctant to fight what could well turn out to be a losing battle. He wasn't afraid to fail.

Like she was afraid to fail.

That was why she'd laughed off Sally's suggestion to go after what she wanted and seduce a larger-than-life man if that's what it took to get it. She was afraid she couldn't do it. Terribly, totally afraid. *But you'll never know for sure unless you try,* she told herself.

And she kept telling herself the very same thing throughout the rest of that afternoon, right up to the time she helped Jordan pick out a good home for his newly acquired plant at one side of the short flight of stairs leading up to his back porch. *You'll never know.*

"Thanks. I'll see you tomorrow night," he said when their project was finished and the hovering basset hound had left them to sniff a path around the yard. Leaning over, Jordan brushed his palms on his denim-clad thighs. ''How about going to that Italian place again?''

She could have easily agreed. Oh, so easily. Instead, she found herself taking a deep breath and saying, ''How about a home-cooked meal for a change? I'll make something.''

Jordan straightened slowly. ''At your house?''

''Mmm-hmm. I haven't made a pot of beef stew for a while.'' And it was something a cook didn't have to watch every minute, something that would allow plenty of time for...other things. Like doing her darnedest to convince Jordan Trask to make love with her.

Which was exactly what she intended to do, Tess suddenly decided, because she could no longer stand being riddled with doubts about her ability to achieve that goal. One way or the other and for better or worse, she had to know for certain. ''You could bring a bottle of wine,'' she said in the most offhand tone she could manage.

For a long moment he just stared at her. Finally he said, ''Okay.''

''Then I'll see you tomorrow at our usual time.'' With that, Tess spun on one heel and headed for the side of the house, where a narrow concrete walkway led to a slatted-wood gate opening to the sidewalk and tree-lined street. Don't look back, she ordered herself, and don't even consider changing your mind.

Tess closed the gate behind her and took firm steps toward her front door, thinking that she had a dinner to plan. Not that the meal itself would present any major problems. Besides the stew, she would fix a fresh green salad, pick up a loaf of crusty bread from the bakery and bake a pie for dessert. No, food was the easy part.

Setting the dining room table for an intimate dinner for two was more of a challenge, she had to concede. Truly intimate dinners, at least for the past few years, had been totally outside the scope of her experience. Still she always kept candles on hand, and there were twin crystal candleholders around somewhere. Hopefully she could find them.

She also had the good china and silverware she used mostly on holidays, plus a lacy white cloth to show both to advantage. Fortunately, fresh flowers for a centerpiece were as close as her garden. Tess nodded to herself. Everything considered, the table would look good enough to pass muster.

But would *she* look good enough?

That was the real question, Tess knew. If she wanted to lure a man, it only made sense that she had to be alluring. Or as close to it as she could get.

Tess mulled the situation over as she climbed the stairs to the upper hall and entered her bedroom. Woken from a nap, the gray cat greeted her with a small yawn and a full stretch across the middle of an ivory comforter.

She put her hands on her hips. "Don't just lie there, Roxy, my girl. Help me figure out how I'm going to get sexy enough in twenty-four hours to pull this off."

Roxy merely yawned again.

"Some help you are."

With a resigned sigh and the undeniable knowledge that she was on her own, Tess walked over to her closet, slid back the mirrored door and studied her choices. To her narrow-eyed gaze, there were depressingly few items in her wardrobe that could be described as anything approaching alluring. Comfortable, yes. Glamorous, no.

Sexy? Not hardly.

Then her gaze settled on a simple fitted sleeveless sheath with a matching jacket, both of lightweight aqua linen. She'd bought it for a summer wedding two years earlier and hadn't worn it since. With the high-collared jacket securely buttoned, the dress was decorous enough to satisfy even the most conservative of maiden aunts. Without the jacket…

Well, it had possibilities, Tess decided, tapping one finger to pursed lips. Given her options, this was probably the best she could manage on short notice. At least it would display some skin—as much as she'd feel comfortable displaying at this stage of things, at any rate. And a pushup bra—which she had, although she seldom used it—would guarantee some cleavage at the edge of the V-necked bodice, or as much cleavage as she could come up with.

Throw in a tasteful amount of jewelry, add a trip to the drugstore to renew her sadly diminished makeup supplies, and she'd wind up looking a little like a femme fatale. Maybe. It was, she thought, worth a try.

And while she was visiting a drugstore, she'd better pick up something else, common sense told her in no uncertain terms. It might mean going out of her way to shop somewhere where she wasn't a familiar face, which meant nowhere in the immediate vicinity, but she knew she'd be downright foolish not to have protection available.

Just in case.

Just in case things worked out as she planned. Just

in case she managed to achieve her goal and take a temporary lover tomorrow night. Just in case she got a certain man's hands out of his pockets. And on her.

Finally.

JORDAN SAT on his back porch steps, one strong fist closed around a cold can of cola and a frown firmly in place. This Friday was turning out to be a far cry from what he'd expected that morning, he had to admit. He'd been looking forward to spending time with Tess the following evening, but now he was definitely of two minds about the whole situation.

True, he'd be getting a home-cooked meal, and he couldn't say that was all bad, especially since he wasn't much of a cook himself. There was no denying, though, that the time he'd be spending with his neighbor was hardly what he'd been planning on. Some food and friendly conversation in a busy restaurant was one thing. An unexpected invitation to share a quiet dinner at the house next door was another matter entirely.

She'd thrown him a curve, no question about it.

"And now I have to deal with the fact that we'll be alone for hours," Jordan muttered to himself. "Looking and not touching is going to be a damn sight harder under those circumstances."

Jones, who was lounging at the bottom of the steps, offered what his owner chose to take as a sympathetic growl.

Appreciating the support, Jordan craned his neck back and downed a short swallow of his drink. He no longer doubted the wisdom of adopting a dog, not when this one was turning out to be such a good companion. Yes, he'd definitely done the right thing there.

What he did have doubts about, though—and a lot of them, he couldn't deny—was his decision to take home a plant that was on the verge of extinction.

In the red-tinged light of the setting sun, Jordan switched his gaze toward one side of the steps and dropped it to the object in question. He hoped to heaven he hadn't done more damage by moving the thing, but he had to confess, at least to the more candid parts of him, that it looked in even worse shape than it had a few hours ago.

Leaning forward, he brushed one finger over a sadly limp leaf. *Why in the world had he said he'd take it when he didn't know squat about growing things?*

He'd been asking himself that ever since he'd brought the plant back to his place. Unfortunately, he had yet to come up with a reasonable answer. Probably because there wasn't one. And if he had the choice to make all over again, he had more than a hunch that he'd do exactly the same thing.

"Whatever the case, and whether I'm crazy or not for tackling this, you're here with me and Jones now," he told the plant with quiet firmness, "and I don't want you to even think about checking out on us, buddy. No way. You've got a job to do and a crop to bring in. I plan on tasting some homegrown tomatoes before this summer is over."

He also, Jordan thought, planned on eating dinner at the house next door and getting out of there as quickly as courtesy allowed. Hopefully, it would be quick enough to keep him from making a big mistake.

His hostess wasn't on the menu. Not tomorrow

night. He had to remember that, because if he hauled in his hormones and bided his time, it could only improve his chances of starting an affair with Tess Cameron.

Eventually.

Chapter Five

Something told Jordan he was in trouble the minute his neighbor opened her front door and greeted him with a wide smile of welcome. Major trouble, it said, because only a brief, tip-to-toe glance was necessary to note that she looked different tonight, different enough to put some of the more basic parts of him on full alert. In an automatic response, he tightened one hand around the wine bottle he held and slipped the other into a side pocket of the olive chinos he'd paired with a white cotton shirt sporting long sleeves rolled up to the elbows.

''Come on in,'' she invited softly, stepping back to let him enter. She shut the door behind him and snapped the lock closed with a quiet click.

Had he imagined it or had her voice been a little huskier than normal? he wondered, venturing another look her way. One thing for sure, he'd never seen her wearing anything resembling what she wore this evening, a dress the color of an island pool in the tropics. Not only did it show a length of leg and outline gently curving hips, it was also cut low enough in front to display some creamy flesh he'd be far better off not seeing.

So quit looking while you're ahead, Trask, and don't even think about touching.

Jordan cleared his throat and hastily raised his gaze past a moist, rosy-pink mouth to meet clear blue eyes. For some reason they seemed bigger tonight under thick lashes that certainly looked darker and longer. "I didn't realize this was a dress-up occasion," he said.

Tess waved that statement away with a flutter of pink-tipped fingers. "It isn't. I just thought this outfit would be a cooler option on such a muggy night."

He couldn't argue with that. It was definitely on the sultry side, and the dress probably would be cool, since it didn't cover all that much of her. Not that he was looking. As of right this minute, he wasn't letting his eyes dip below a silky-skinned neck, no matter what.

"Let's go into the living room and relax," she suggested, still smiling that same smile. "We can open the wine and have a glass before dinner." With that, she led the way toward an arched door on one side of the hall, her high heels tapping softly on the tiled floor.

The room they entered held a deep green sofa and two overstuffed chairs covered in a bright floral fabric. Twin brass lamps rested on cherry-wood end tables that matched a low coffee table. In the background, the strumming strings of a Spanish guitar mingled with a steady Latin beat.

Jordan suspected it was some sort of south-of-the-border dance tune. Which dance exactly, he couldn't be sure. He did know it wasn't a staid waltz. Or anything close.

Fixing his gaze straight ahead, Jordan firmly resisted the urge to see if curvy hips were tempted to sway to the pulsing beat as he followed his hostess across the room. Time to start a casual conversation, he told himself. After quickly searching for a subject, he took refuge in the most ordinary of all—the weather. ''That was some storm we had earlier this afternoon, wasn't it?''

Tess tossed him a backward glance that sent small silver hoops at her ears swinging below gleaming brown curls. Unless he missed his guess, she'd done something to make her hair look even shinier than it usually did. Then she batted those thick lashes so many times he figured she might have something in her eye. When her smile didn't falter, though, he decided there was no real problem.

''Nature provided quite a show,'' she agreed in that same husky tone. ''The radio forecast said we'll probably get treated to another one before the evening's over.'' As if to prove that to be right on target, thunder rumbled for a moment in the distance. ''Have a seat. The sofa's comfortable. I'll get a corkscrew and you can open the wine.''

He sat down at one end of the long sofa and placed the wine bottle on a cork coaster set between two crystal glasses resting on the coffee table. Keep the conversation going, he flat out ordered himself as he pretended great interest in the color-splashed cover of a gardening magazine topping a half dozen stacked at one side of the footed glasses. *And keep it casual.* ''You know, my phone went out during the storm and still wasn't working when I left to come over here.''

Her voice drifted back to him as she walked away. ''That probably means mine's out, too. I haven't tried to make any calls today.''

He was still bent over a cover photo featuring a field of flowers in full bloom when she came back into the room a minute later. "Something smells good," he said in the heartiest tone he could summon even as kept his head down.

She laughed a throaty laugh. "I'm not sure if that's the stew or my cologne. Probably the stew, though. I doubt you'd get a whiff of what I'm wearing unless I got a lot closer."

He didn't even want to think about her getting closer. But that's exactly what she did as she propped a hip on one arm of the sofa practically at his elbow and handed him the corkscrew. In the blink of an eye, he got a good whiff of that cologne. Floral laced, yet somehow smelling like pure sin as well, it hit him squarely in the gut and had him concentrating so hard on his task that he had the bottle open in record time.

"Do you like it?" she asked softly.

"I've never tried it, but it's supposed to be a good vintage."

"I meant my cologne."

For an instant he stilled completely, bottle in hand. "It's, uh, nice." Figuring that was as neutral as he could get, he continued to pour the rich, red cabernet.

"Sally gave me the cologne for my birthday last year. It's called—can you believe it—Forbidden Fantasy."

He could believe it, wouldn't have been a bit surprised, in fact, if it was guaranteed to make a man fantasize about any number of things, all of which were probably banned in one place or another. He knew he could come up with a few dandy ones right now—if he'd let himself.

Forbidding his head to turn a notch, Jordan raised

a hand and offered a glass Tess's way. "I can't wait to eat dinner," he said as she took it from him.

But what he really couldn't wait for, he reflected grimly as he lifted his own glass for a steadying swallow, was for a meal that was bound to be torture to be over so he could go back to his place and take the edge off with a cold shower, another in a recent and seemingly endless string of them. It was beginning to occur to him that he was in danger of forgetting what warm water felt like. Maybe he'd rediscover its comforts sometime. But not tonight. He was dead sure of that.

He should have dug in his boot heels yesterday and insisted on their going to a restaurant this evening. Hell, he should haul them both to one right now. And he'd do it, too, if it wouldn't have his hostess coming to the logical conclusion that he was downright insane. *Maybe you'd be better off, Trask, if you stopped talking and just kept drinking.*

Jordan decided to take that advice.

As silence settled over the room, broken only by the throbbing beat of the music, Tess draped one arm across the back of the sofa and sipped her wine, wondering what in the world she had to do to get her guest's attention. Either Jordan was acting strangely tonight or she was a complete dud as a femme fatale. Whatever the case, she could hardly deny that he seemed to be doing his best to ignore her. She also had to admit that she was getting a little irritated. More than a little, truth be told.

So she wasn't drop-dead gorgeous? So she didn't ooze sex appeal out of every pore? *So what?* None of that meant he shouldn't at least have the good manners to look at her when she talked to him.

Thunder rumbled again, this time louder than before, and Tess's irritation rose right along with the wind that began to rattle the windows. Finally she had had enough of being treated as if she didn't exist. She would, she decided, win a certain man's attention even if she had to strip down to bare skin in the middle of the living room to get the job done.

And then maybe she'd throw him out.

Leaning forward, she set her glass down on the coffee table with an audible click. Then she turned and deliberately aimed every bit of cleavage she had directly at Jordan's chiseled profile. "Dinner will hold for a while," she said in the most come-hither whisper her vocal chords could produce. "Right now I have a taste for...something else."

He turned his head then, slowly and carefully. And looked. And stared. It took every ounce of willpower she had not to move a muscle while he gazed long and hard at the shiny silver pendant firmly settled in the vee of her breasts. At last he raised his eyes, inch by inch, until they finally locked with hers.

"Are you by any chance," he said very softly, "trying to seduce me?"

That was when Tess did something she had never done before in her entire life. She lost her temper completely.

Prompted by pure outrage, she surged to her feet, took a quick step back from the sofa and all but roared her reply. *"Of course, I'm trying to seduce you.* Why do you suppose I went to all this trouble?" She held her arms straight out to indicate herself. "And as if that wasn't enough," she added, forging on, "I did everything I could think of to stir things up around here. I'm playing *tangos,* for heaven's sake.

"And *you,*" she summed up, pinning him with a glare, "have the nerve to tell me you can't wait to eat dinner!" She didn't think about what she did next. She just grabbed the top magazine from the stack on the table and flung it at him.

Hazel eyes wide, as if he couldn't quite believe what was happening, Jordan dodged the magazine and let it whiz by his ear. Then, blowing out a rough breath, he set his glass down with a clunk and rose in one swift motion. "Well, that does it. Do you know how long I've been—"

"Ready for your next meal?" Tess finished in a huff before launching another magazine straight at a broad chest. This one hit with a solid thud and fell to the floor.

His own temper flared in his gaze as Jordan jammed his fists on his hips. "No, ready for you," he shot back. "Ready, willing and damn eager, as a matter of fact."

Now her eyes went wide as thunder boomed directly overhead. In a flash, the lights went out and the music died in midnote. "So why didn't you do something about it?" she asked, her voice abruptly quiet in the sheer darkness. She couldn't see a foot in front of her, but had no trouble feeling the sudden tension snapping in the air between them.

"Because I thought *you* weren't ready," he replied, his tone all at once as quiet as hers.

She took a deep breath. "I'm ready."

Those two words were all it took to get his hands on her. She quickly discovered the truth of that when strong arms came out of nowhere and locked around her. They gripped her tightly as a firm mouth came down on hers. And then words suddenly seemed irrelevant as she readily parted her lips in surrender to a silent demand.

This time he kissed her exactly as he had the first time, and she welcomed the heady onslaught to her senses, the thrilling threat to her ability to think at all. Once again, the ground seemed to rock under her feet. She fisted her hands in soft cotton covering a hard chest, both to steady herself and to tug the man who held her closer still, until there wasn't a breath of space between them. And all the while, she kissed him back with everything she had, determined to do her best to demonstrate that she was every bit as ready, willing and eager as he.

It was Jordan who eventually broke the heated kiss. He lifted his head and breathed in, then released the air in a rush and breathed in more. "I hate to mention this," he got out at last, "but I'm not totally prepared for where this is headed. Before things go any further, I've got to run back to my place and get something."

Tess's mouth curved at the tips. "No, you don't," she was pleased to inform him. "I made a trip to the drugstore this morning. I had to drive miles out of my way to keep the whole thing private, but we have everything we need."

His low chuckle in response to that news was definitely on the wicked side. "So you did intend to seduce me."

"You'd better believe it." She made her way down the side of a newly shaved jaw with a string of small kisses and took in its sandalwood scent, then nibbled lightly on a corded neck and sampled its tangy taste. "How am I doing?" she asked her guest before tugging his shirt out of a narrow waistband and sliding her hands up a muscled back.

He sucked in a ragged breath. ''Consider yourself well on the road to success.''

When he returned the favor by running his tongue around her ear, oh-so-slowly, and then carefully biting on the lobe, it was her turn to meet the challenge of keeping her lungs in working order. It wasn't easy, not when the ground had started rocking again. ''I'm not sure how much longer I can stand up,'' she said.

After another wicked chuckle, he murmured, ''Luckily, you don't have to.''

Jordan got them both to the sofa, blindly making his way and managing to do no more damage in the process than hitting the edge of an end table hard enough to rattle the lamp it held. Soon he was stretched out full length, the sofa's deep cushions under him and Tess lying on top of him. Just where he wanted her, he reflected with satisfaction even as he clenched his teeth to hold back a groan at the feel of her body flat against his.

He could no longer look, he thought. At least he couldn't see nearly enough in the murky darkness blanketing the room. But he was free to touch—finally—and he would do his damnedest to take every advantage of it.

With that goal firmly in mind, he started at the warm, smooth tops of delicately boned shoulders and gradually worked his way down, letting his hands be his eyes, taking his time when he couldn't deny that certain increasingly demanding parts of him would have far preferred some fast action. Not that they were getting it, he told himself. The soft-skinned woman he planned to explore inch by inch might well have no objection to hurrying things along, but that didn't mean she didn't deserve a little seduction on his part.

He intended to give it to her.

Now his hands slid over a trim waist and down the gently curved hips he had mightily avoided watching earlier. He squeezed them lightly on his way to firm thighs still covered by crisp linen. And there his patience slipped.

Because he suddenly had to, he pulled the dress up as far as it would go in one quick motion and put his hands on the slender legs he badly wanted wrapped around him. It didn't take him long to discover that the silky nylons covering them ended at midthigh, held in place by something he was dead certain every hormone-driven male fatally attracted to the female half of the population had dreamed about—maybe even drooled over—at some point. Jordan had to admit he was no exception.

He cleared his throat. "You deliberately wore a garter belt to drive me crazy, didn't you?" Despite his efforts, the words still came out hoarse.

Tess placed her hands on his shoulders and levered herself up on her forearms. He couldn't see the angle of her mouth as she looked down at him, but he clearly heard the smile in her voice. "I hope you like it. Sally gave it to me last Christmas. It's, ah, scarlet-red."

He swallowed, hard. "You don't say."

"Mmm-hmm. And mostly made of see-through lace…what there is of it."

Jordan did groan then, long and heavily. He was, after all, he reminded himself, a mere man. "Remind me to thank your friend for her generosity the next time I see her. Right now, I vote we put dinner on the back burner, stumble our way upstairs to your bedroom and—''

He never finished that statement, stopping in midsentence as his ears, attuned to the slightest sound after months of training followed by years of sheer necessity, picked up what he was all but certain was the small grating noise signaling a key sliding in the front-door lock. With his rough-skinned palms still curved around far softer thighs, he automatically braced himself as the lock turned and the door creaked open.

From above him, Tess suddenly issued a quiet gasp and tightened her grip on his shoulders, as if she'd just become aware of the fact that they had a visitor. And then they both froze as someone shouted out a cheerful greeting.

''Mom, I'm home!''

IN WHAT SEEMED LIKE a lifetime later to Tess, but was actually only scare seconds after a familiar voice had made a totally unexpected announcement, she and Jordan were on their feet and trying to right their clothing—hardly an easy task, Tess discovered to her dismay. Since it was still pitch-dark, they bumped into each other more than once, although both managed not to grunt out loud at the impact of stray elbows.

''Where are you, Mom?'' her daughter called again from the direction of the hallway.

''I'm in the living room, Ali,'' she called back, struggling to keep her voice calm while her hands fumbled in the effort to wrench her dress down to her knees. ''Are you okay, honey?''

"Sure. The doorbell didn't work, so Gram used the key you gave her. She said it was because the electricity's out. We saw how the whole block was dark when we drove down the street. It'd be way cool on Halloween."

Tess resisted the urge to sigh as her brain finally kicked in and informed her that of course her mother would be with Ali. Of course!

You have to get your act together right now, Tess, she told herself, knowing full well that little got past Glenda Fitzgerald. If she didn't want her mother to know what had been happening on the sofa—and about to happen upstairs—she had better do her darnedest to put on a convincing performance. Trouble was, she'd never won any rave reviews in her high school drama-club productions. In grammar school, her specialty had been playing trees. She'd been good at that.

"Are *you* okay?" Jordan murmured at her ear. His warm breath gently fluttered the hair at her temple and reminded her of exactly how okay, indeed all-out wonderful, she'd felt until seconds ago.

"I'm fine," she whispered in reply, though she was a long way from sure it was true. Then again, she had to be fine. She didn't have time for hysterics. She drew in a steadying stream of air, thanking her lucky stars that at least the lights were out at the moment.

And that was when the lights came on.

Tess blinked in the sudden brightness, then braced herself and aimed a resigned look across the room. The first thing she saw was her daughter standing in the arched doorway, small lips curved in a wide grin that happily displayed twin dimples. The next thing she saw was her mother, who stood a step behind and studied the scene before her with shrewd dove-gray eyes.

After a hastily tossed glance over her shoulder found Jordan looking as cool and collected as she'd have given a small fortune at that point to appear to be, Tess stepped forward and forced a smile. It was show time.

Ali, decked out in well-worn jeans and a striped blue-and-white shirt featuring a railroad logo on a front pocket, met her in the middle of the room for a hearty hug. "Did we surprise you, Mom?"

"Yes, you did." Which had to be the understatement of the decade, Tess silently tacked on, gazing down at her much-loved child. "This is a long way from San Diego, pumpkin."

Ali's brisk nod of agreement had shoulder-length brown braids briefly dipping toward a narrow chest. "But we got here pretty fast. Just put pedal to the metal and kept on truckin'."

A phrase she'd learned from her grandfather, Tess knew. Which brought another thought to mind. "Where's Grandpa? Didn't he come with you?"

Ali's voice abruptly dropped to a confidential level. "I think Gram has to talk to you about that."

A sudden chill ran down Tess's spine before she realized that nothing could be seriously wrong with her father. Ali's greeting had been far too cheerful. No, it had to be something else, she decided. Glancing up, she met her mother's gaze, which continued to assess the situation.

No one had ever accused Glenda Fitzgerald of being dense, Tess thought. Or dowdy. Her casual coral cotton blouse and matching slacks showed off a still admirably firm and fit figure. Her dark blond hair, naturally wavy and cut stylishly short, was the same color it had always been, even if it did need a little help to maintain that flattering shade now that she was in her fifties.

Summoning another smile, Tess made her way over for a hug. Enfolded in graceful arms that had lost none of their gentle strength, she inhaled a familiar lavender scent before catching sight of a trio of suitcases standing in the hall. The smaller two she recognized as Ali's; the much larger one could only belong to her mother. It was, she couldn't help noting, a far cry from an overnight bag.

Tess considered saying *It's good to see you* as she took a half step back, found she couldn't because at the moment it just wasn't true. ''Why didn't you let me know you were coming?'' she said instead. Which, she admitted, was one doozy of a question.

Glenda blew out a softly exasperated breath. ''I've been trying to call you since this morning.''

Tess considered what she'd been doing earlier that day, or more specifically what she'd been buying. She willed herself not to blush. Thankfully, her cheeks remained cool. ''I had some errands to run this morning,'' she said, ''and then the phones went out after a storm blew through this afternoon.''

Knowing that she couldn't put off something any longer, she turned back toward the living room and the man who still stood where she'd left him. ''I'd like you to meet someone, Mother.'' She went on in the most casual tone she could muster to introduce Jordan as her new neighbor.

Much to her relief, he played his part admirably as Glenda shook hands and gave him a long once-over. ''Your daughter was kind enough to invite me for dinner,'' he said matter-of-factly, as if that were the beginning and end of it.

Glenda gazed past him toward one of the end tables and the tall lamp whose pleated white shade now hung at a rakish angle. With a keen, sweeping glance she went on to plainly take in the sight of the thick magazine propped up on the back of the sofa, where it had landed after missing Jordan, as well as another lying spread open on the cream-colored carpet. ''It looks as though a small storm also blew through here,'' she said dryly.

''Things got a little confused when the lights went out,'' Jordan explained with a totally deadpan expression.

''Hmm,'' was Glenda's sole response to that statement.

Judging it time to break in, Tess introduced Ali next, and Jordan hunkered down for another handshake, this one accompanied by his crooked smile. ''I'm pleased to meet you,'' he said, his voice turning soft and low. ''I understand you plan on making your mark in the world of trains.''

It won him a smile in return. ''Yep. I'm gonna drive a locomotive and blow the whistle, too. One of the boys in school said girls can't do that, but I told him he was full of it—like my grandpa would say.''

Jordan nodded. ''I think girls can do just about anything they put their minds to. Well, maybe except snort, spit and scratch, all at the same time.'' His mouth curved in a wry quirk. ''Guys seem to have that one pretty much locked up.''

''I bet I could do it if I tried,'' Ali replied on a giggle. ''Grandma says I'm a tomboy.'' It was a proud declaration.

Jordan studied an outfit that was light-years from gingham and lace. ''My guess is that she's right.''

A bemused expression settled on Tess's face as the conversation turned to sights seen on the drive from California. Despite the frantic events of the past few minutes and the fact that her nerves were still nowhere near calm, she watched the easy exchange of words between man and child through a mother's eyes and found her heart warming in response. *Maybe too much,* something inside her suddenly cautioned.

Her expression sobered as reason told her that warning voice could well be right. Just because a thoughtful effort was being made to relate to an eight-year-old, and its maker seemed to be enjoying the task he'd set for himself, didn't mean anything had changed. Not, Tess thought, when it came to an undeniable conclusion reached on the very day a far-from-ordinary man had leaped over a fence and into her life.

Jordan Trask would be gone when the summer was over.

She remained convinced of that. So regardless of how physically close they became, it frankly wouldn't do to get too emotionally involved. Not that she could ever be intimate with a man she didn't like and respect. She knew herself more than well enough to know that. Right from the first, she'd been attracted to her new neighbor for those very reasons.

But liking a man for the person he was and respecting what he'd made of himself was one thing. Handing her heart over was a whole different matter. Doing anything so foolish could only be a mistake. She didn't doubt that for a second, and didn't question the wisdom of keeping it firmly in mind.

Just then another round of thunder boomed, and now rain lashed at the windows, starting to come down in earnest as the lights flickered ominously. For a moment, no one spoke. Then Ali's voice bubbled out, sounding a long way from frightened. "Boy, it's too bad it's not Halloween! Is the whole block gonna get dark again?"

Jordan straightened to his full height. "Could be. I think we'd better light a few candles, just in case."

"Mom's got lots of those," Ali informed him.

He looked at Tess. "Where do you keep them? A flashlight might come in handy, too, if you have one."

She told him where to find both, plus matches. As he left for the kitchen, Ali gave a little sniff. "Something smells yummy, Mom."

Tess realized it was not a reference to her cologne. Thank goodness. "It's stew, honey."

"Good. I'm hungry. Gram and I stopped for hamburgers and milk shakes, but that was hours ago."

"Why don't you go upstairs and wash your hands before dinner, dear?" Glenda suggested ever so casually.

Being far from dense herself, Tess quickly deduced that her mother wanted to talk to her alone—and the conversation was probably going to be anything but casual. She swallowed a resigned sigh as Ali promptly fell in with that suggestion and started for the hall.

"I have to see Roxy, too," she told them, moving with the sheer energy of youth and already at a half run. "I wonder if the storm scared her."

Tess shook her head. "You'll probably find her lounging on your bed, not cowering under it."

One thing Tess knew for certain was that the cat

wouldn't be in her bedroom. She had deliberately closed the door earlier to make sure an empty bed would be available—for all the good it had done both her and the man she'd intended to lure there. "Nothing fazes that cat," she added staunchly, determined not to reveal the disappointment she couldn't help feeling.

She wouldn't be taking the temporary lover she still badly wanted to take. Not tonight.

Her daughter's well-used running shoes pounded their way up the stairs and Tess was left to deal with her mother, who aimed another pointed glance down at the wine bottle and glasses still standing tall on the coffee table. A minor miracle, Tess decided, everything considered.

"Did Ali and I interrupt something?" Glenda asked, once again looking at Tess.

She quickly countered that question with her own, reminded of the old saying that the best defense was a good offense. "Where's Dad?"

As a diversion, it achieved its purpose with startling speed. Glenda dropped her eyes in a flash, then took a deep breath and slowly returned her gaze to her daughter's. "I suppose there's no easy way to say this...."

"Say what?" Tess prompted at the hesitation, even though she was beginning to believe that she didn't really want to hear what was coming. Not at all.

"Okay," Glenda went on at last after taking another breath. "I'm not usually one to beat around the bush, as you well know, so I'll just come out with it." She squared her shoulders. "Tess, I've left him."

Stunned in spite of the fact that she'd steeled herself for trouble, Tess felt everything inside her clench as a single word rang in her mind. *Drastic.*

Ali had overhead her grandmother threatening to do something...drastic. Apparently, Glenda Fitzgerald had done exactly that.

Oh, Lord.

Although she knew the answer full well, Tess found herself asking anyway. "Left who?"

Her mother stood firm and looked her straight in the eye. "Your father, of course."

"YOUR MOTHER DID *WHAT?*"

"Left. My father, that is. I just tried to call him, but the phone's still out."

Jordan frowned as he struck a long match to light twin ivory candles standing at opposite ends of the dining room table, the last of several he now had burning brightly around the first floor of the house. "Weren't they getting along?"

Tess added the required place settings, thinking that her intimate dinner for two was about to become a family event. Fortunately, she had plenty of stew. Unfortunately, she'd totally lost her appetite. "Apparently there's been some tension lately. My mother seems to be upset by a lack of attention on my father's part. At least that's as much as I was able to find out while I got her settled in the guest bedroom."

"I'm sorry." Jordan flicked out the match with a quick snap of his wrist. "All things considered, would it be better for you if I made myself scarce?"

Tess shook her head. "You were invited for dinner, and I intend to feed you." She paused. "I guess I should warn you, though, that you might want to leave while you have the chance. I doubt the rest of the evening is going to be all that upbeat.''

One edge of Jordan's mouth rose as he faced her across the centerpiece she'd created, a shiny silver bowl filled with a vivid mix of fresh flowers. ''I suppose I'm tough enough to handle it.''

The wry comment made Tess smile her first truly genuine smile since she'd welcomed him at the door full of plans to knock his socks off. ''I do believe you are tough enough.''

''Thanks for the vote of confidence.'' All at once something sparked to life in hazel eyes, something that jangled her pulse in spite of everything. ''This isn't over, Tess,'' he told her. ''It's just to be continued.''

To be continued... She liked the sound of that. Yes, she definitely did.

Things might not be so bad, she thought. Maybe her parents' marriage wasn't in all that much trouble. Maybe her mother would soon view things differently. Maybe.

''Did I tell you how much I like that dress?'' the man who studied her added.

''No,'' she replied, deciding not to remind him of how he'd ignored it earlier.

''Well, I do. It looks great.''

Her spirits rose right along with the brow she lifted. ''Even with the jacket on?'' she asked.

Raising a hand, she fingered a high pearl button securing the stand-up collar. After leaving her mother to freshen up in the upstairs bathroom, she'd made a quick trip to her own bedroom before returning downstairs, aware that—circumstances unfortunately being what they were—cleavage had become the last thing she needed to display.

Jordan nodded slowly. "I have to admit that with the jacket that outfit is less of a threat to my blood pressure." *Since I can't get my hands on you,* his gaze added silently.

But she heard the words as clearly as if they'd been spoken. "We wouldn't want you to blow a gasket," she said solemnly, tongue in cheek.

Just then the sound of fast footsteps signaled her daughter's return trip down the stairs. Her mother, Tess knew, wouldn't be far behind. Lord only knows what would follow.

As if he'd read her mind, Jordan's tone turned firm. "We'll get through this meal one way or the other," he told her.

And they did.

At least by the time Ali asked for seconds, Tess was beginning to believe they just might make it through dinner without any further references to the scene her mother had walked in on earlier. So far the conversation had run along far different lines, chiefly because Ali could talk a mile a minute and plainly wasn't aware of any undercurrents lurking in the cozy room brightly lit by a small crystal chandelier overhead.

"Anyone else for seconds?" Tess asked, having finished ladling out more stew from a china tureen for Ali.

"I'll take you up on that," Jordan replied from his seat across the length of the table, where Tess had chosen to place him with her mother and daughter sitting on opposite sides between them. He rose and walked toward her, a gleaming ivory plate ringed with silver held in one large hand.

"You seem to have a hearty appetite, Mr. Trask," Glenda said softly, twirling the stem of her wineglass between slender fingers tipped with clear gloss.

Uh-oh, Tess told herself as she gave Jordan another helping. There'd been the barest hint of innuendo in that remark, just enough to put her on edge.

"Yes, Mrs. Fitzgerald, I do," Jordan agreed mildly. He accepted the refill and resumed his seat.

"Please call me Glenda," she added, matching his tone. "We may as well be on a first-name basis, since I'll probably be in Harmony for a while." She lifted one shoulder in a shrug. "Who knows? Things being as they are, it could be for some time."

Hardly thrilled with that news, Tess was even less delighted by the fact that some little ears very dear to her were in hearing distance. The last thing she wanted was for Ali to be upset by what was happening. She aimed a pointed glance at her daughter, which her mother clearly caught.

"I've already explained to Ali," Glenda said calmly, "that I'm taking a break from living with her grandfather."

Ali paused with a heaping forkful halfway to her lips and nodded thoughtfully, as though she had already mulled it over and decided to take the situation in stride. "I guess a break is okay," she said, "but I told Gram I don't think Grandpa's gonna like it."

As if to underscore that statement, the front door, which no one had thought to relock after the evening's earlier frantic events, suddenly creaked a loud protest as it was opened far from gently. A near slam soon signaled its closing before heavy footsteps stomped their way down the hall. The man who abruptly appeared in the doorway to the dining room didn't waste time with preliminaries. He just growled out a grim announcement.

"This nonsense is over. I've come to get my wife."

Chapter Six

Jordan leaned back in his chair and kept a wary eye on the broad-shouldered, big-boned man who had just stalked into the house sporting a stormy expression as dark as one of the clouds passing overhead. True, the rest of him was colorful enough—bright plaid shirt, rust-colored pants and tan leather loafers, all topped by a mustard-yellow baseball cap. But none of that lightened the tight cast of his features.

Under other circumstances, Jordan knew his instincts would have urged swift action in response to the abrupt entrance of someone who, although probably close to sixty, looked entirely capable at the moment of wreaking total havoc. Rather than remaining seated, he'd have been on his feet and confronting the intruder—would be now, if he'd had any doubts about the new arrival's identity.

"Hi, Grandpa," Ali called from her place at the table, her cheery welcome breaking a short, tense silence and confirming what Jordan had already figured out.

Tess's voice followed hard on the heels of her daughter's. "Hello, Dad," she said on a resigned sigh. "You're just in time for dinner." Then, as if to forestall any further outbursts, she wasted no time in adding, ''You can also meet my new neighbor, Jordan Trask.''

That statement brought the irate man up short. Obviously, he'd been too busy being royally ticked off to notice his daughter's guest, but that changed in a heartbeat as a probing glance aimed around the room rapidly landed on the sole stranger in sight.

There was no doubt about where Tess got her blue eyes, Jordan thought. Her father's were slightly darker, but not a whit less intelligent. That was crystal clear by the way an almost laserlike gleam sparked to life as they studied him.

Jordan slowly rose and walked toward the hall door as Tess completed her hostess duties by introducing Frank Fitzgerald. ''Glad to meet you,'' Jordan said, and extended a hand. One every bit as large as his was raised to complete a firm handshake.

''Same goes for me, uh, Trask,'' the other man replied haltingly, his low voice a deep rumble. Being taller than average as well as no lightweight, he had to raise his strongly formed chin just a few notches to meet Jordan's gaze. ''You're a neighbor?'' he asked even as he removed his rain-dotted cap and raked blunt fingers through thick chestnut-brown hair liberally sprinkled with silver.

Jordan nodded, recognizing a strained stab at making polite conversation when he heard it. ''I recently rented the blue frame house next door.''

Frank's ruddy-skinned forehead creased in a frown. ''That's old Miss McKinley's place.''

Tess walked up to them. ''Not any longer, Dad. Miss McKinley passed away peacefully a few months ago after a brief stay in a nursing home, remember?''

"No," Frank replied after a slight hesitation. "I don't think I ever heard about it."

Tess shrugged. "Well, I spoke to Mother on the phone shortly after it happened. I assumed she would—"

"I did," Glenda said briskly, breaking in. "You can tell your father, Tess, that I mentioned it to him the same day you called, but he was probably too busy channel surfing to pay me any mind...*as usual.*"

Frank scowled and launched an exasperated look at the woman still seated at the table with her back firmly facing the doorway, her spine as straight as an arrow and as stiff as a steel post. "You can tell your mother, Tess," he bit out, his tone just as brisk and to the point, "that a person can't always remember everything that's said to him."

Jordan decided it was time to take his seat and stay out of the line of fire. Another of Tess's sighs followed him as he walked back to the table. This one was long and hard.

"Why don't you sit down, Dad," she suggested, "and have some stew?"

"Guess I might as well," her father muttered after a second's consideration.

"You can take Ali's place," Tess told him. "She's done with her dinner. She can have dessert upstairs and watch television in her room."

"Goody," the girl tossed in. "What's for dessert, Mom?"

"Apple pie. I baked one this afternoon."

"Awright!" Ali pushed back her chair and dropped her gaze at the sound of a loud meow of protest coming from the gray cat stretched out at her feet. "Nap time's over, Roxy. We get to watch TV in bed. And I get to eat pie.''

Another long meow rose up in response to that last comment, this one louder still.

''Okay, you get a bite of the crust.'' With that concession, Ali picked up her well-cleaned dinner plate and angled a look at the man seated beside her. ''Do you like apple pie?''

Jordan allowed that he did as he broke off a small hunk of French bread, deciding that the midnight-dark eyes viewing him with the simple directness of a child had probably been handed down to Ali from her late father. For the first time, he found himself considering what he knew about the man who had lost his life at such a young age. Not much, he had to concede.

But something.

He hadn't forgotten the way Tess had hesitated after mentioning the accident that had made her a widow, as if there might have been more to it. But how much more and exactly what was involved, he had to wonder. Assuming, of course, there actually was more. And not that it was strictly any of his business, he reminded himself.

Unaware that he'd been considering anything beyond food, Ali stepped closer and leaned in. ''Ask for an extra big slice,'' she advised in a whisper. ''My mom's pie is yummy.''

''Hmm. It wouldn't hurt to have her teach you how to make it someday,'' he murmured, keeping his voice low.

Ali grinned. ''I will—after I learn to drive a train and toot the whistle.''

He dipped his chin in a nod. ''Sounds like a plan to me.''

In the minutes that followed, Jordan concentrated on finishing his dinner while his hostess got her father settled at the table and sent her daughter off with a generous helping of pie and a plump cat for company. A wary silence soon descended on the dining room as small footsteps quickly thumped their way up the stairs to the second floor.

Jordan couldn't help recalling that if the evening had gone differently, he and Tess would be upstairs right now, working up an appetite in her bedroom and satisfying another one at the same time. As things stood, he was still hungry enough to growl a protest even louder than the cat's, and no amount of food was going to satisfy it, or him. Not hardly.

He'd told Tess the truth when he'd said her prim and proper jacket was currently a blessing to his blood pressure. But he hadn't mentioned how his pulse still wanted to take off on its own every time he found himself thinking about a certain red garter belt. If he wasn't careful, the thing was going to drive him crazy before he'd even seen it.

And he would see it, he promised himself as he watched the woman wearing the garment in question produce a wineglass for her father before resuming her seat. Sooner or later—and the sooner, the better—he'd get his hands on that scrap of lace again, Jordan vowed. Not to mention its owner.

Wiping out thoughts of something sinfully scarlet, Jordan took up the host's role for a moment and polished off the wine by filling the new arrival's glass to the brim. He had to admit Frank Fitzgerald looked like someone who could use a stiff drink about now. Unless he missed his guess, the big man was coming to the grim conclusion that getting his wife back might not be so easy. Judging by the way Glenda had totally ignored her husband since he'd sunk down in the chair opposite her, Jordan had to allow that Frank was probably right on target with that one.

"Thanks, Trask," the older man muttered as he grabbed up his wine. He took a long swallow and set the glass down. "I needed that. After all, it's not every day a man discovers his wife has left him by finding a note tacked on the refrigerator door."

Glenda lifted a gracefully arched eyebrow at that disclosure but didn't make a sound.

It was Tess who issued a quiet gasp. "Goodness gracious," she murmured, staring at her mother with wide eyes, as though she couldn't believe it.

"Don't looked so shocked, dear," Glenda advised, speaking for the first time in minutes. "It could well be that I tried to break some news this morning only to have it go right over a particular person's head." She paused. "Hardly surprising, I suppose, since there was a ball game on at the time. Still, one might have expected a slightly more earthshaking reply than, 'That's nice,' followed by, 'Do we have any potato chips?'"

Dead silence reigned for a stark second before Frank turned to Jordan. "It was the highlights of the '69 World Series, for crissake!"

The tension in the room zinged to new heights, and Jordan told himself that if he were a smart man, he'd keep his mouth shut right now. And he did.

Failing to find an ally in the only other male present, Frank switched around and looked at his daughter. "I've worked damned hard for most of my life. Now that I'm semi-retired, I have a right to watch TV and a relax a little, don't I?"

Tess shot a speaking glance at Jordan, as if to say *how do I get out of this one?* ‘‘Well, Dad,’’ she said at last, ‘‘I suppose there are two sides to most everything.’’

Frank blew out a heavy breath and dropped a brooding stare down at his plate. He shoveled in stew for a few hushed minutes, then set his fork down with a soft clatter. ‘‘What I want to know is, how long is this nonsense going to go on?’’ he ground out, reaching for his wine again.

Long since finished with her own meal, Glenda sat back and aimed a puzzled gaze around the table, which managed to take in everything but the man facing her. ‘‘Did someone just say something?’’ she asked, oh-so-innocently.

Frank snorted.

Tess rolled her eyes.

Jordan cleared his throat. ‘‘I think, ah, somebody was wondering how long this, er, situation was going to continue.’’ He knew he probably should have kept out of it, would have for sure if he hadn’t been too downright curious about the answer to Frank’s question himself.

Glenda nodded. ‘‘Well, if *somebody* is really interested and the *situation* is the state of my marriage, I have to say that I see no reason to return to living with a man who snores like a buzz saw, never remembers to put the toilet seat down and has the shape of the TV remote permanently indented in his hand.’’ She folded her arms under her breasts and lifted her chin a lofty notch. ‘‘Why the devil should I put up with him any longer?’’

Nobody had a ready answer for that one.

BY THE TIME dessert was over and Glenda had left for the guest room with a final comment to the three still seated at the table about expecting to get a good night's rest sleeping alone, Tess was ready to pull out every strand of the hair she'd gone to great pains to fuss over earlier that day. At least she was tempted to dig in with her fingers and give it a few good yanks. As disasters went, the family dinner she'd just survived gave a whole new meaning to the phrase *man the lifeboats.*

Even worse, her parents' marriage was floundering and could well be in danger of winding up on the rocks. Certainly nothing had been settled between them tonight. Which was hardly surprising, Tess had to concede, given that the parties in question weren't even talking directly to each other. Her mother was plainly in no hurry to change that situation, either.

For his part, her father was still brooding to beat the band, like a bear nursing a sore paw. And to put the final cap on the whole evening, Tess knew she was going to have to find a tactful way to mention sleeping arrangements, because one thing was evident: her parents would not be sharing a bed tonight.

Tess finished the last of her after-dinner coffee and watched Jordan make small talk with her father, chiefly about the weather and how it could affect the electrical and telephone service in outlying areas even more than in major cities. Neither man looked all that enthusiastic about the discussion, but at least at the moment things were going better. Too bad she had no choice but to get something straight, and soon. Tactfully, though, she reminded herself.

She waited for a break in the conversation, then propped her elbows on the table and summoned a small smile. "Dad," she said, "you must be tired after that long drive and, ah, everything. Provided the phone's working now, why don't I try to get you a comfortable room at one of the bed-and-breakfasts in town?"

Despite his daughter's deliberately soothing tone, Frank frowned in a heartbeat. "Does that mean I'm not welcome to stay here?" he asked bluntly.

"Certainly not," Tess quickly replied, groping for patience.

"Then what in blazes does it mean?"

So much for tact, she thought. She let out a breath and decided to be a little blunt herself. "It means, I'm sorry to say, that there are three bedrooms in this house and all of them will be occupied tonight."

Her father's firm mouth twisted in a rueful grimace. "And what makes you think things will be different at any place to stay in town on a weekend in the middle of summer?"

Unfortunately, she didn't have a reassuring response for that one, knowing as well as any Harmony resident that summertime brought visitors in full force hoping to catch a few mountain breezes while escaping big-city living and the sizzling heat of lower-lying desert areas for a while. "I can at least try," she said. "There may have been a last-minute cancellation."

And if she wasn't successful, she decided, her father could always sleep on the sofa in the living room. Trouble was, that was bound to turn into a bit too much togetherness come tomorrow morning. As deeply as she loved her parents, she didn't even want to consider the prospect of watching them continue to conduct their own personal Cold War over the breakfast table. She couldn't help but think that what they needed was a little breathing space.

She also couldn't help but think about what had happened on the living room sofa hours earlier. To have her father sleeping in the same spot tonight where his daughter had been doing her best to seduce a man was hardly likely to give her any comfort while she tossed and turned in her own bed. And she would be tossing and turning. She knew that without a doubt. Everything inside her was still a long way from calm.

So try calling the bed-and-breakfasts, Tess, and you might get lucky. She was poised to do exactly that when her father spoke again.

"Maybe I should just go back to San Diego," he grumbled, "and wait for your mother to come to her senses."

Those words still hung in the air when the other man at the table set down his coffee cup with a quiet clunk. In the next breath, and for what seemed like too many times to count that day, Tess heard someone make a totally unexpected announcement.

"I have two extra bedrooms," Jordan said, his voice low, his tone mild. "Why don't you stay with me?"

JORDAN AND THE MAN who had agreed to become his houseguest left the small garage at the rear of Jordan's rented property and made their way across the backyard. The powerful storm had finally blown its way through, and bright stars dotting a dark sky now blinked overhead. A cool breeze provided a sharp contrast to the earlier muggy dampness heavy in the air.

"This is damn decent of you, Trask," Frank said, trudging along with an easy grip on a nylon gym bag retrieved from the trunk of the car he'd just parked next to Jordan's SUV. "Offering a bed to someone who's more or less a stranger isn't something everyone would do."

"Don't give it a second thought," Jordan replied, meaning every word. As far as he was concerned, he deserved little praise for his offer to act as host. It had not, he knew full well, been a strictly charitable act on his part. Not even close. Hell, he'd been prompted by his own self-interests, pure and simple, having come to the swift conclusion, upon hearing a gruff reference to a possible return to California, that the last thing he wanted was for Frank Fitzgerald to leave Harmony right now without Glenda Fitzgerald willingly in tow. It didn't take a genius to figure out that starting an affair with Tess Cameron would be difficult—if not downright impossible—as long as her eagle-eyed mother was around.

So he had a houseguest.

Frank stopped on his way up the back stairs. He glanced over one side of the wood railing and slowly shook his head. "I have to say that, even as dark as it is, I'm pretty sure that's the sorriest excuse for a tomato plant I've ever seen."

"It'll shape up," Jordan replied firmly, dropping his gaze to the object in question. At least, maybe because the stairs provided some shelter from the wind, it didn't seem to be in any worse condition after today's second round of wild weather than it had after the first. It looked much the same as it had the day before, in fact. Which wasn't saying a whole lot, he had to admit.

Barking began at the sound of the men's footsteps crossing the porch floor. "That's Jones," Jordan explained as he unlocked the back door. "It's okay, pal," he added in a reassuring tone as he pushed the door in. A soft glare spilled from the kitchen, where he'd left the light on.

"It's just me," he told the dog. "And I brought some company."

The basset hound greeted Jordan as if he'd been gone for a year rather than a few hours. He couldn't help but smile as he watched a furry tail wag like windshield wipers on high speed. He also couldn't deny that he continued to find himself a little amazed by how easily this animal had settled into totally new surroundings while his owner was still gradually adapting to an entirely different way of life.

"Nice dog," Frank remarked when Jordan finished a short introduction. Bending, the older man gently scratched behind one long ear and won a grateful growl for his efforts.

"Looks like you've made a friend," Jordan said, thinking that if he'd had any major doubts about Tess's father, the dog's quick acceptance of the big man would have put them to rest. However Glenda felt about her longtime husband, Frank plainly had some good points, maybe more than he seemed to be getting credit for at the moment. One thing for sure, anyone who drove a classic kick-butt '68 Camaro in flaming orange couldn't be all that much of a dud.

Right now, though, his guest still looked as if he could use a stiff drink. One glass of wine clearly hadn't done the trick. All things considered, Jordan figured he could use a dose of something stronger himself.

"You can take whichever of the spare bedrooms you want," he said. "Why don't you get settled in while I pour us both a nightcap in the form of some good brandy?"

For the first time that evening, Frank's mouth curved up at the corners. "You're a prince, Trask."

Jordan shook his head. "Not hardly. Princes have a lot to live up to."

He didn't think the other man would be so quick to call him one either, not if Frank had walked in on the same scene Glenda had. At least there was one plus to the two parties not speaking to each other, Jordan decided. For the moment at any rate, Frank wasn't likely to find out that his daughter and her friendly neighbor had nearly been caught taking getting-to-know-you to new heights.

After Frank left to choose an upstairs bedroom, Jordan let Jones out to do his nightly duty and poured generous servings of aged liquor into two small glasses. The dog scratched softly on the door just as Jordan returned the squat bottle to the cabinet over the sink.

"Didn't want to stay out there long tonight, did you?" he said, acting as doorman. "Come on, pal, let's go into the living room and wait for our company."

Jones soon got comfortable on the navy rug while Jordan chose a well-padded swivel rocker covered in faded turquoise brocade. It could be older than he was, yet it bore his weight with ease.

It wasn't long before Frank joined them, casting an appraising gaze around the room as he walked in. "I'd be willing to bet that Mabel McKinley, rest her soul, never met a shade of blue she didn't like."

"Seems so," Jordan readily agreed, picking up one of the glasses set on a small wooden end table standing at his side. It had hardly escaped his notice that most of the house was decked out in tones ranging from sky-blue to deep-ocean. "Here's your brandy."

Frank accepted the offering, issuing a quick thank-you, and made himself at home on the cobalt-striped sofa. He downed a short swallow of his drink, then sat back and propped an ankle on a knee. "This place seems to have its share of antiques, too," he said, aiming another look at twin pearly ceramic lamps with fringed shades and a large quilt with a peacock design at its center decorating one long wall.

Recognizing it as more small talk, Jordan could only be grateful. If Frank chose to avoid mentioning his private problems, his host was more than willing to oblige. As a marriage counselor, Jordan knew his skills amounted to zip. And right now, after a dinner that had turned out to be anything but normal—not for him, thank God—he'd just as soon have to deal with a wounded mountain lion as a hassled husband.

"I suppose the television could also be termed an antique," he drawled as his guest's eyes landed on the old set encased in sturdy walnut standing on the floor across from the sofa.

Frank shot him a glance. "Does it work?"

Jordan nodded. "As it happens, it does. A minor miracle, I'd say, and a good thing, since it's the only TV in the house." He paused for a beat. "Of course, it dates back to the time before remote controls."

For a second, the older man actually looked appalled. "No remote," he repeated slowly. Then he raised his glass and downed another swallow of brandy, this one a lot longer than the first.

Jordan had to bite back a grin, thinking that one of Glenda's complaints about her husband could soon start disappearing. Through no choice of his own, Frank just might lose that indentation in his right hand. Too bad he had to come all the way to Harmony to do it.

And too bad, Jordan thought, that he, himself, wouldn't be spending the night where he still badly wanted to spend it—in a surprisingly seductive woman's bed.

TESS TOSSED and turned that night, exactly as she'd expected, and found herself wide-awake at the crack of dawn the next morning. Normally the optimistic side of her nature would have had her looking forward to a new day. At the moment, though, another side of her firmly said that she'd be far better off throwing the sadly rumpled covers over her head and lying low for as long as possible.

But that, she knew, would solve nothing, so she threw back the floral-print sheet and got out of bed, sending the ruffled hem of her white cotton nightgown to settle around her ankles as she reached toward a nearby chair for her yellow terry-cloth robe. The fabric was as frayed in spots as she currently felt, but it was as reliably comfortable as an old friend, and she had no intention of parting with it.

Right now, she'd gladly take any sort of comfort she could get and be grateful for it.

After a quick stop in the bathroom, Tess considered the merits of jump-starting her system with some caffeine, decided as she made her way down the stairs and into the kitchen that some hot herbal tea minus the caffeine might be a wiser choice. Her nerves could probably use a break, she had to admit, since they were none too calm after yesterday's events. At least she wouldn't have to watch her parents face each other over the breakfast table. Not this morning.

Thanks to Jordan.

Tess couldn't deny that she remained a little amazed by his unexpected offer. To take in someone he'd just met—and hardly under the best of circumstances, to boot—certainly went beyond the bounds of common hospitality. She hoped he wasn't regretting the invitation, then decided he just might be, as a glance out the kitchen window found the man in her thoughts standing on his back-porch steps, a mug of something held in one hand. He wore gray sweats and sported a frown deep enough to make out at a distance, even among the strands of dark hair hanging over his forehead. To her mind, it appeared as though he hadn't slept any better than she had—and he wasn't happy about it.

Tess abandoned her plan to make tea and let herself out the back door. Once he caught sight of her, Jordan stepped off the porch and met her halfway at the fence dividing their yards. Now she had no trouble noting a night's growth of dark beard, giving his chiseled features a dangerous cast. And a sexy one.

"Good morning," she said as lightly as she could manage, all things considered.

"Morning," he muttered in reply, his tone a bit rougher around the edges than normal.

Maybe it was just his morning voice, Tess told herself. Or maybe he was feeling even grumpier than he looked. Remembering how tact had recently failed with another man, she opted for candid honesty. "I had a devil of a time trying to get any sleep last night, and it seems as though you did, too.''

''I'll say. Your father *does* snore like a buzz saw,'' Jordan wasted no time in informing her. ''It was more than loud enough to hear right through the wall between our bedrooms.'' He blew out an aggrieved breath. ''I'm beginning to see your mother's side of things, believe me.''

Tess lifted a wry brow. ''So you weren't thinking about me? It was just Dad's racket that kept you up?''

Jordan did smile then, briefly and ruefully. ''Hell, no, I wasn't thinking about you.'' He lifted a hand and raked it through his already well-mussed hair. ''I was just driving myself up the wall imagining everything that might—no, *would*—have happened if your folks were still sleeping together. Back, I might add, in California.''

For some reason, that made her smile herself. It was on the shaky side, true. But she felt more cheerful than she had in several long and frustrating hours.

Even grumpy, Jordan clearly still wanted her as much as she wanted him. And that was good. The problem right now was doing something about it.

''We've got to get things back on track,'' Jordan added firmly, as though he'd read her mind.

''You're right,'' Tess promptly agreed. She wrapped her fingers around one of the white slats separating them and ran her tongue over her lips. ''But probably the only way to accomplish that anytime soon is to—''

''Get your folks back together,'' Jordan finished for her. ''Don't I know it.'' He set his mug down on the narrow flat rail near the top of the fence. ''That's why I intend to start on that project this morning.''

Tess's eyes widened in a flash. One more totally unexpected announcement, she thought, wondering how many that made in the past two days. "*You're* going to play matchmaker?"

"No, we are." Jordan reached over the fence, cupped one hand around the back of her neck and tugged her upper body toward his. "I'll work on your father. You do the same with your mother." He lowered his head until their lips were a breath away. "Does that sound like a plan to you?"

"Definitely," Tess managed to get out before his mouth locked with hers. Then he kissed her exactly as he had the first time, exactly as he had the evening before. Exactly as she craved for him to kiss her and needed to kiss him back.

Finally he lifted his head, released his hold on her and looked her straight in the eye. "To be continued," he said. And then he picked up his mug, whipped around in a flash and marched back toward his house, looking for all the world like a man primed to do battle.

Knowing that she now had her own battle to wage, Tess could only hope to heaven that they both could claim victory. And soon.

AFTER SHOWERING and shaving, Jordan was better prepared to face the day as he headed back down to the kitchen. He refilled a dog dish for a clearly grateful Jones, poured himself another cup of coffee and put breakfast fixings on the counter. Then he sat down at an old-fashioned, farmhouse-style oak table set in one corner under curtained windows overlooking the backyard and considered his plan of attack.

Lord knows, he was still no marriage counselor.

Just the idea was laughable, he told himself. He'd never been married, never even given any serious thought to making that kind of commitment. His own upbringing had provided little in the way of incentive to explore the possibilities of a family lifestyle after he'd reached adulthood, that was for sure. He wasn't particularly against marriage—or in favor of it. He definitely was no expert on the subject, though, not by any means.

But he had to do something.

Jordan was still mulling things over when Frank all but stumbled into the kitchen, wearing only a short-sleeved undershirt draped over his rust-colored pants and looking pretty much as Jordan figured he, himself, had looked earlier that morning. Not exactly Brooks Brothers material. But then, most men probably needed a shave and shower to look halfway human. Women, on the other hand—and most especially one woman, he'd recently learned—could look downright delectable with tousled curls and not a scrap of makeup.

"Help yourself to some coffee," he told his guest, indicating the pot on the counter with a wave of his hand. "There's also juice, cereal, toast, and whatever else you want to put together."

Mumbling his thanks, Frank bent to give Jones, whose tail was again wagging a mile a minute, a companionable scratch behind the ears. That project completed, he filled a mug with dark brew, then walked over and sank into a ladder-back chair across from Jordan. The dog wasted no time in following and stretching out at one side of the table.

"Did you sleep well?" Jordan asked mildly.

"Yeah, more or less," Frank replied in another mumble.

Jordan sat forward and launched what he'd just decided would be the first skirmish in the coming battle. "Wish I could say the same, but your snoring would do a good job of keeping a dead man awake."

Frank blinked. "Is it that bad?"

"Yes," Jordan him flatly. "Believe me, I'm beginning to feel some sympathy for your wife."

A fast frown creased a ruddy forehead. "Is that so? Got to say that I'm beginning to think I liked you better last night, Trask."

"Just telling it the way I heard it, loud and clear." Jordan propped an elbow on the table. "I'm hardly surprised now that it was the first gripe on a certain woman's list."

Frank hunched his shoulders in defense. "Not much I can do about it. Not when I'm asleep."

"You could try sleeping on your side," Jordan countered. "I seem to remember reading something about that helping."

"I like sleeping on my back."

Choosing to ignore that statement for the moment, Jordan launched another volley. "Was your wife right about the toilet seat, too?"

Frank's mouth twisted. "Do *you* remember to put the seat down, ace?"

"I'm a bachelor," Jordan didn't hesitate to remind him. "I don't have to remember."

"Well, it's not always easy," the older man groused in return. He lifted his mug and took a steady swallow. "Sometimes nothing about living with a woman is all that damn easy, let me tell you."

Jordan decided it was time to get to the point, and he didn't mind being blunt about it. Not at all.

"Do you want your wife back?"

Frank's frown only deepened at the question. "Humph. After the stunt she pulled yesterday, I should probably give that some thought."

"Well, I wouldn't think too long. She's a good-looking lady, Fitzgerald. Don't kid yourself. There are plenty of men who'd be glad to step in and take your place."

"The hell they will! She married me, and no man's going to step into my shoes."

Frank underlined those words by slamming a fist on the table, suddenly looking fierce. Which was by and large the reaction Jordan had hoped to achieve, even if Jones protested the noise with a brief growl.

"Then I think you'll have to shape up," Jordan told the big man, again bluntly.

Whatever Frank might have said next was foiled by the merry chime of the front doorbell. Jordan pushed back his chair and rose to his feet. "It seems we have company. If by any chance a minor miracle has prompted your wife to come over and talk to you, I suggest you consider what you're going to say back." With that, he started for the hall. "Any mention of potato chips would probably not be a good move," he added dryly as he walked out.

But it wasn't Glenda. Instead, Jordan found Ali Cameron standing on his doorstep. Dressed in denim overalls paired with a pink blouse, she greeted him with a grin. "Hi, Mr. Trask. Mom said Grandpa stayed with you last night. Can I see him?"

"You bet." Jordan stepped back to let the girl enter. "I'm sure he'll be glad you came." Which was probably the bald truth, Jordan thought. Frank might well be relieved not to have to discuss his personal problems for a while.

"Since we're neighbors, why don't you call me Jordan?" he suggested, shutting the door.

Ali stared up at him. "My mom says I'm not supposed to call grown-ups by their first name unless we're related. It's...etta-something."

Etta? "Ah, etiquette," Jordan supplied as realization hit.

"Yep. That's it." His visitor pursed her lips. "But I guess I could call you 'Mr. T,' if that's okay."

"All right," Jordan agreed. "Your grandfather's in the kitchen. Let's go find him."

"Your house is made just like ours," Ali said, chatting as they walked down the hall. Mary Elizabeth—she's my best friend in the whole world—has a bigger house, but it doesn't have an upstairs. I like sleeping high up. Do you?"

"Yes." *When I can get some sleep,* Jordan added in a silent grumble, deciding that someone sawing wood all night in the next room definitely didn't help in that department.

But any complaint he had about his houseguest quickly faded when the older man beamed like a beacon at the sight of his granddaughter and readily welcomed her with outstretched arms that closed securely around her as she climbed into his lap and placed a sound kiss on a weather-worn cheek.

Taking in the scene as he stood in the arched doorway, Jordan had to wonder if anyone had ever welcomed him in just that way when he was a child. He didn't think so. Certainly he couldn't remember that ever happening. And he figured he would have remembered.

"How's my freckle-faced angel this morning?" Frank asked, tugging gently on one light-brown braid.

"I don't have that many freckles, Grandpa." Ali rolled her eyes. "I keep telling you."

Frank narrowed his gaze in a mock study. "You have four stretched right across your little nose. That makes you freckle-faced in my book."

Ali laid her head on a broad shoulder. "Grandma says I'll grow out of them."

Her grandfather's expression abruptly sobered as he angled a look at Jordan. "Well, she may be right—" he heaved a quiet sigh "—about more than one thing, I just might have to admit."

Jordan nodded slowly, meeting the other man's gaze for a meaningful moment. "That'd be my guess," he said mildly, thinking that unless he missed his guess, Frank was reconsidering the whole situation and could decide to try to change a few of the things on his wife's gripe list. Needless to say, his host was more than willing to help him in that effort.

A soft whine began just then as the basset hound, clearly determined to finally be noticed so he could receive his fair share of attention from the latest visitor, lifted a paw and placed it on a denim-clad leg. Looking down, Ali smiled a wide smile. "Hi, I'm Ali. Who are you?"

"He's Jones," Jordan said by way of introduction as he resumed his seat.

"I have a cat," she told the dog proudly, then aimed a look at Jordan. "Has Jones met Roxy?"

Jordan ran his tongue over his teeth. "I suppose you could say so. He came up with the idea a while ago that it would be great fun to chase her around your backyard—until she smacked him on the nose and showed him the error of his ways.''

Ali dipped her chin in a nod. ''She's tough.''

''You're telling me,'' Jordan replied with feeling.

The wry comment won him a giggle. ''Mom says Roxy likes me best.''

''Of course, she does,'' Frank said firmly. ''That cat isn't only tough—she's got good taste.''

At that point, maybe deciding he'd heard enough about his nemesis, Jones headed for the back door, where he stopped and issued a quiet bark.

''I'll let him out,'' Ali offered. She hopped off her grandfather's lap. ''Can I go out with him?'' she asked, turning to Jordan.

''I don't see why not,'' he replied. ''There's a Frisbee under the porch steps. Jones is a whiz at playing catch.''

As Ali left, readily following Jones out the door, Frank took another long swallow of his coffee and quickly seemed lost in thought.

Deciding to let the older man mull things over, Jordan sat back and looked out the window just in time to see Ali pause on her way down the steps. Somehow it didn't surprise him when she dropped her gaze to the scrawny plant he'd brought home and slowly shook her head.

What did surprise him, though, was how much he—a man who'd had little contact with children—found himself drawn to a small girl with midnight-dark eyes, a freckled nose and more than her share of ambition. He had to admire that last point. Once he, himself, had been filled with determination and plans to make the world a better place. Maybe Ali would be more successful in her efforts. He hoped so—*really* hoped so—because he had to admit that he not only admired Ali Cameron, he downright liked her.

Just don't let it go too far, Trask, the more practical parts of him said. And he couldn't deny that keeping some emotional distance was the way to go, given that he had no idea how long they'd even be neighbors. Right now, the future still held more questions for him than answers. One thing he knew full well, though, was that coming to care too much for one little girl could backfire on him.

Trouble was, he had to wonder how much choice he was going to have in the matter. *Not a helluva lot,* another less practical but maybe wiser part of him silently contended.

Jordan figured he'd just have to wait and see.

Chapter Seven

"And then when I finished playing with Jones, I opened the door to go back inside and Grandpa and Mr. T were still sitting at the table, making a bet about the funniest thing. It was the *toilet seat.* Every time one of them leaves it up, they have to pay the other one ten whole dollars." Ali switched her gaze back and forth between her two companions. "Honest. They shook hands on it and *everything.*"

Tess straightened in her chair and aimed a speaking glance at her mother across the breakfast table, where a late-morning Sunday brunch was still in progress against a backdrop of sparkling sunshine that cheerfully streamed in through the windows. Up until a second ago, she'd been taking in her daughter's recount of an earlier visit to the house next door with half an ear while stifling a sleepy yawn and silently debating how best to pursue a certain joint matchmaking project. Now, after that last startling disclosure, she was wide-awake and her ears at full attention as Ali went on.

"Then Grandpa told Mr. T that they'd have to try something else with the snoring, because he wasn't gonna fork over any money for what he did in his sleep. Mr. T agreed with that," Ali continued after an instant's pause, "but then guess what?" Her young forehead creased in a puzzled frown. "He said it was a downright blessing his TV's too old to have a remote, because at least they didn't have to worry about that one."

All Tess could think was that the grumpy male who'd seemed so determined to succeed at the crack of dawn that morning knew how to wage a battle. When Jordan decided to do something, he obviously didn't waste any time. He was, as she'd found herself concluding soon after meeting him, a man of action.

"Then Jones ran past me into the kitchen, and Grandpa and Mr. T stopped talking." Ali polished off her bacon and cheese omelette with a last gulp. "It was weird."

Glenda cleared her throat delicately. "Well, perhaps not weird, dear, but certainly interesting, although I have to say it's not strictly polite to listen in on conversations. Then again, I don't suppose you could have helped hearing."

"Nope." Ali reached for her milk and finished it in one quick swallow. "Can I call Mary Elizabeth, Mom, and let her know I'm back?"

Tess, who could only be glad that Ali had been around to listen in this particular case, told her daughter to use the telephone upstairs and soon the two adults were left alone at the table. For several ticks of the kitchen clock, neither spoke. Finally Tess lifted a brow and said, "I wonder what they'll try to do about the snoring."

The wry comment had her mother's coral-tinged lips curving, just as she'd hoped it would. Unfortunately, that slight smile faded a moment later as

Glenda sat back and released a soft sigh. "I suppose I should wish them luck. Heaven knows, I haven't been very successful lately at trying to get your father to do something about anything."

Tess pushed aside an ivy-trimmed stoneware plate still half full and leaned in. "That may be true, but it seems as though he's willing to make an effort now."

"Could be," Glenda acknowledged, meeting her daughter's gaze. Dove-gray eyes suddenly lit with a bright, probing glint. "It also seems as though Jordan Trask might be a man of many talents."

"Not really," Tess replied after taking a short second to catch up with the swift switch in subject. She deliberately kept her tone mild. "He's hardly the greatest dancer in the world, for instance, and—"

"Dancing?" The gleam in Glenda's gaze hiked up a sharp notch. "Hmm."

Uh-oh. "We danced together once at Sally and Ben's annual summer party," Tess explained. Which, she told herself, was the total truth. She didn't have to mention how it had felt being held in those strong arms.

"He's not much of a gardener, either," she added, forging on while she had the chance. "Heck, the man probably doesn't know a hoe from a hole in the ground." *But he knows how to kiss—and how.* "Still," she summed up, "I'll admit he appears to have managed to open Dad's eyes to a few things."

"Maybe," Glenda allowed, raising a tawny and clearly skeptical brow. "It's early days yet."

Grateful that the subject of her neighbor had apparently run its course—for now, at any rate—Tess decided not to waste any time in switching things back to the matter at hand. "Will you at least start talking to Dad again? I think he deserves that much."

"We'll see," her mother replied after a long moment.

"He's a good man, Mother."

Once again, Glenda sighed softly. "That was never in doubt, Tess. The question is—is he a good husband?"

The only person who could truly provide the answer to that one was the woman seated across from her, and Tess resisted the urge to issue a sigh of her own, this one long and hard. It was almost a relief when the phone hanging on the wall above the counter rang, although it stopped before she could make a move to respond. Swift seconds later, Ali's voice, raised to a near shout, came from upstairs.

"Mr. T's calling for you, Mom!"

"All right," Tess called back, telling herself that she shouldn't let her pulse jump at that news. It jumped anyway. "Put the phone on hold and I'll get it in the kitchen."

"Okay!"

After a brief glance at Glenda, who now seemed fully occupied in dealing with the half-eaten omelette and sliced fruit remaining on her plate, Tess walked over and picked up the receiver. "Hi," she said by way of greeting.

"Hi, yourself," Jordan replied evenly, sounding a lot more upbeat than he had earlier.

Maybe he'd already won the first round on that bet, Tess mused. It wouldn't have surprised her.

"How are things going on your end?" he asked in the next breath.

''Not as well as I'd like,'' Tess admitted, but she kept her tone as light as she could.

''Hang in there,'' he advised, then paused for a beat. ''Got any plans for dinner tomorrow night?''

Tess hesitated, biting her lower lip. ''Things being as they are,'' she said carefully, fully aware that her mother was well within hearing distance, ''I don't think I should be making any.''

And she couldn't deny the truth of that. As much as she might want to, probably the very last thing she needed was to go off on a date alone with Jordan. Not now, when someone steps away was already wondering—and not just a little—about her relationship with a certain man.

''Hopefully, a home-cooked meal will change your mind,'' that man proceeded to tell her, ''because your father and I are inviting your entire household over for dinner at my place.''

''Oh.'' *What in the world,* Tess thought. Then realization bloomed and had her lips quickly tipping up at the corners. ''Ah, yes, that's an entirely different situation.''

''I had a hunch you'd think so,'' Jordan murmured, as though he were up to speed on the reason for her earlier hesitation. ''Do you suppose you can *all* make it over here tomorrow after you get home from work?''

''Yes,'' she replied firmly with a quick glance back at her mother. ''Don't worry on that score.''

Even if she had to drag one stubborn woman every step of the way, they would all be there, Tess vowed. ''What's on the menu?'' she added, dropping her voice to a low murmur as she leaned against the counter.

A short silence followed before Jordan said, ''I figured I'd, ah, barbecue some ribs.''

''Mmm, sounds great.'' Tess paused as something occurred to her. ''Do you have a charcoal grill?''

''No.''

Now she had to grin. ''Want to borrow mine?''

''I thought you'd never ask.''

BY THE TIME his houseguest had been with him for several days, Jordan could only hope to heaven that if he ever so much as considered playing matchmaker again, someone would give him a swift, hard kick in the butt to remind him of what he'd gone through the past week.

It would, he decided, be an act of mercy.

Hosting a dinner had been only the beginning of the whole thing, though it had certainly been a memorable start, given that Frank Fitzgerald's cooking skills had turned out to be as shaky as his own. Between the two of them and the mess they'd made, another storm powerful enough to roar through and take out the entire kitchen would have been a definite plus at the end of that particular evening.

True, Glenda had finally started talking to her husband on Monday. But as the week wore on, it had become clear during the course of a few other shared meals at Tess's place that the sharp-eyed woman was only giving up silence in favor of softly spoken, yet pointedly barbed comments aimed squarely at the man she'd married.

''And now, pal,'' Jordan said, dropping a glance down at his companion, ''I get to go out on a Friday night double date with a couple who anyone in their right mind would hardly vote at the moment most likely to live happily-ever-after.''

Tongue hanging, Jones panted out a short round of canine sympathy as he lounged on the bedroom carpet and watched his master dress for the occasion.

''At least I'll be with Tess,'' Jordan muttered as he tucked his white T-shirt into the waistband of well-worn Levi's. And the date *had* been his idea, he reminded himself, one born of sheer desperation after deciding that if Tess's father wound up with no wife to impress with the changes, there was little point in the shaping-up effort Frank was making.

And, to the big man's credit, a devil of an effort was being made. Jordan knew that to his personal cost, since he was currently down twenty bucks in the toilet seat betting pool. On the other hand, he was finally getting some sleep, given that the snoring had come to a quick stop once they'd come up with the plan to tie one of Frank's arms to the side of the headboard to keep him from flopping over onto his back in bed. Last night, after stacking some pillows behind him, they'd left both arms free, and blessed silence had still reigned.

Thank God.

As far as the television was concerned, after hopping up and down to switch channels during most of his first day as Jordan's guest, Frank had eventually decided it just wasn't worth the trouble and had since rediscovered the joys of watching the sunset from the back-porch steps while his granddaughter told him about her day.

Family, Jordan thought. That was what rested rock solid at the core of this particular man, he more than suspected. Frank was hardly the type to wear his heart on his sleeve, but when all was said and done, his family meant more to him than anything. It would be a damn shame if his marriage didn't make it.

Jordan had barely come to that last conclusion when the old-fashioned phone set on an even older pickled-oak nightstand rang. He leaned over and picked up the receiver. "Trask here."

"I know you're there, friend," said a low voice tinged with a Western drawl, "although I still can't figure out why you're hibernating in Happyville."

Jordan flashed a smile, recognizing that voice with no trouble at all. "It's Harmony, and things aren't as dull around here as you might think, flyboy."

As an agent who doubled as a helicopter pilot for the Border Patrol, Ryan Larabee had spent much of the past several years blazing a trail through the sky, which seemed to suit him to a tee, Jordan reflected. Still the lanky man with the laughing eyes had never lost the knack for planting his tooled-leather boots soundly on the ground and cocking a black Stetson at a rakish angle, a tribute to his cowboy upbringing on a ranch in Wyoming.

Ryan chuckled deep in his throat. "I'm guessing your definition of *dull* and mine wouldn't exactly match."

"Maybe," Jordan allowed. "As I remember, you always liked a walk on the riskier side of things even more than I did."

"True."

Jordan could all but see a familiar cocky grin forming with that last word. "Still raising hell on a regular basis?"

"Most every chance I get," Ryan drawled, and

paused for a beat. ''How are you making out these days?''

Jordan realized it wasn't a casual question, despite its being issued in the mildest of tones. Ryan Larabee was only one of several people who had tried to talk him out of resigning. Where some had been more concerned for his career, though, he knew Ryan had been worried about him personally. He was one of the few real friends Jordan had made in his life.

''I'm doing fine,'' he said firmly.

''Got a handle yet on what you're going to do next?'' the other man asked, again mildly.

''No,'' Jordan admitted. ''But I have the whole summer to make a decision.'' *Right now, I'm busy trying to imitate a marriage counselor,* he thought, and didn't say. Instead, he said, ''For the moment, I'm taking it one day at a time.'' It was true, too. The frustration concerning the future eating away at him before he'd come to Harmony had eased considerably.

Ryan released a quiet breath that might have held a hint of relief. ''Well, I've got to say you sound mighty good, friend.'' He hesitated before continuing, his tone all at once turning far more sober. ''Wish I didn't feel obliged to ruin your day with some bad news.''

Frowning, Jordan asked, ''What is it?''

''Basically, it's a bunch of bull-crap, as far as I'm concerned,'' Ryan gritted out. ''The criminal justice system, being sometimes as contrary as a two-headed mule, let Felix Raine go scot-free today.''

Jordan's mouth twisted. ''I take it a judge threw out the earlier conviction on a technicality.''

"Yep. Raine waltzed out of prison after serving only nine months."

"When it should have been twenty years," Jordan finished, shaking his head. "And that was just for the drug smuggling. We all had a hunch he was involved in more than that."

"But you were the one he threatened to even the score with someday," Ryan reminded him.

Jordan shrugged. "Yeah, the guy liked to talk big, but you know as well as I do that type is usually all talk. It wasn't the first—or last—threat somebody aimed my way while I was on the job, and every one has turned out to be so much hot air."

"Could be this one will, too," Ryan allowed, "but I thought I'd pass along the info anyway."

"Thanks." Another small smile curved Jordan's lips. "If you get tired of pulling stunts with that chopper, flyboy, and decide to take a break, you're welcome to pay me a visit."

Ryan chuckled again. "I don't think Happyville and I are exactly made for each other, friend."

"It's Harmony...and you just might learn to like it."

Jordan's smile was still in place when he set the receiver in its cradle. He couldn't deny that he sometimes missed the company of a few of the agents he'd worked with—the cowboy who loved to fly, most of all. But that didn't mean he would even consider returning to his old job. He'd made the right decision. He was still convinced of that.

Just then, heavy footsteps made their way down the hall and stopped at the open door of Jordan's bedroom. The man who now stood there wore crisp new jeans and a fitted navy T-shirt, both of which Jordan had talked him into buying, since Tess's half of a jointly formed plan for tonight had been the idea to try to spark memories of the days when her parents were dating. Luckily her father was still trim enough to pull off the kind of outfit he might have worn in high school.

"You're looking good, Fitzgerald," Jordan said, and watched a sly grin slowly spread across a broad face.

"I'm feeling good, Trask. I just found the toilet seat standing tall. You owe me another ten bucks, ace."

"Damn."

DEWITT'S DINER HAD BEEN a part of Harmony for nearly fifty years. And it was one of the best parts, many older residents contended, having spent a considerable portion of their younger days and hard-earned money there. Now a firm fixture of a downtown area that held many longtime businesses but no high-rise buildings to compete with the tall pines and low mountains surrounding the city, the diner occupied a one-story white brick structure on the corner of First and Main.

A wide plate-glass window at the front of the restaurant held a neon sign urging passersby to "Try Our Taste-Tested Malts," and a soda fountain with a string of red-topped chrome stools near the door did a brisk business. Red vinyl booths lined opposite sides extending to the rear of the building, and in one of them Tess studied the oldies-rock selections offered by a small wall-mounted jukebox and wondered if it had been such a good idea to come here, after all.

Things were not going well.

But then, she'd had no clue until they were halfway through the burgers and fries everyone had ordered that Henry Dewitt, who'd recently returned to town to manage the diner upon his octogenarian father's retirement, had once had a thing for Tess's mother. Which would hardly have mattered, Tess thought, except the still attractive and undeniably charming Henry had apparently never gotten over it.

"Isn't he the dearest man?" Glenda asked, looking younger than her years in a scoop-necked tangerine top paired with a tan wraparound skirt. The question came after the sandy-haired manager had stopped by for the third time to politely inquire if everything was to their satisfaction—and to reach down and pat Glenda's slender hand with a perfectly manicured one of his own.

"He seems nice enough," Tess dutifully replied, since no one else seemed inclined to answer. Silently she wished one more time that she were sitting on the outside of the booth. Or better still, that her father was occupying that spot, with her mother beside him and away from the aisle. And Henry. Unfortunately, Glenda had wasted no time in sliding in next to her daughter on their arrival, leaving Jordan with no choice but to slide in on the opposite side, with her father taking the last spot beside him.

"I always suspected he had a crush on me when we served on the committee to plan our senior prom," Glenda said, spearing a French fry, "but he never asked me out."

"That's because you were going steady with me," Frank muttered before swallowing another bite of his half-pound burger. "And because," he went on, "though I'd already graduated, I never made any secret of the fact that I was a rough-and-tumble guy going to technical school who wouldn't appreciate anybody trying to horn in on my territory." His tone said that hadn't changed. Not at all.

Glenda smiled far too sweetly. "Ah, yes, that does take me back. Despite school and with both of us working part-time, we managed to do a lot together, didn't we?" She lifted a brow. "Sometimes even something on the spur of the moment, and maybe even a little bit wild, just for the heck of it." Her tone said she had scant hope of that ever happening again.

The edgy quiet following, broken only by a doo-wop group easing out a soulful ballad, had Tess longing for her daughter's easy chatter to fill the gaps. But Ali was happily spending the night with her bosom buddy Mary Elizabeth. So Tess waded in.

"The food's good, isn't it?" she said, directing the comment to Jordan, who met her gaze with a level look that told her he was no more pleased with the way things were going than she was.

"Yes, it is," he agreed mildly, "though I have to admit I've never seen a cheeseburger deluxe served with carrot curls and carved radishes on the side before."

Frank harrumphed. "Obviously the pretty boy's trying to fancy up the joint." No one questioned who he meant by that statement. "After he left town for bigger things, he probably got a higher education waiting tables in the kind of place where *deluxe* means the inflated prices—not the food."

Glenda set her fork down and leaned back, folding her arms under her breasts. "Wherever he learned his good manners, he certainly has them. And everything tonight was delicious.'' She didn't hesitate to tack on the compliment firmly—or to repeat it just as firmly, if more graciously, when the solicitous Henry hurried over to clear away her plate. Deprived of a slender hand he could easily reach this time, he leaned in and patted one creamy upper arm left bare by Glenda's sleeveless top, offering a patent try at the most charming of smiles as he looked down at her.

And that was precisely when Tess saw her father lose it.

JORDAN MANAGED to hustle his group out of the restaurant and into his muscle-black Explorer without giving Frank the chance to make good on his threat to pound Harry Dewitt into the ground, although the big man continued to mutter what might have been a string of curses under his breath most of the way to the Mountain View Drive-In. At least, Jordan thought, pulling into an open slot in the last row of the outdoor theater, Tess was where he wanted her—sitting next to him. That left the Fitzgeralds in the back seat, where a surprisingly quiet Glenda seemed to be considering recent events with thoughtfully pursed lips. As far as her husband was concerned, Jordan had no trouble making out the still-grim set of his houseguest's features in the rearview mirror, despite the growing darkness.

''Popcorn or soda, anyone?'' he asked. ''I'm making a quick trip for snacks before the show starts.''

Frank just shook his head in reply.

Glenda issued a polite, ''No, thank you.''

Tess said, ''I'll go with you,'' and even beat him out in her hurry. ''I need a break from the double date from hell,'' she added dryly, smoothing an edge of a plain white T-shirt that matched his own as they walked toward the refreshment stand.

Deciding they were out of sight of her eagle-eyed mother, Jordan caught her hand in his. "I could use a kiss myself to ease the pain," he said, mirroring her tone. He aimed a glance at the crowd of cars around them, most of which were probably filled with curious Harmony residents. "But I don't suppose that's on the agenda right now."

Despite everything, an amused twinkle lit in the blue eyes that peeked up at him. "We'd probably get more attention than the movie."

Jordan didn't doubt that for a second. "What's playing, anyway?" He hadn't even thought to look when he'd paid the attendant. At that point, he'd still been too busy being grateful that Henry had chosen good customer relations over calling the cops. That would have been a truly memorable end to the evening, bailing Tess's father out of jail.

"Friday is Old Movie Mania night," Tess informed him. "We get to watch John Travolta strut his stuff in *Grease*."

Jordan released a mock sigh. "And here I've been pining to see Godzilla flatten Tokyo one more time."

Tess smiled widely, just as he'd hoped she would. It'd be a long enough evening with the way things were going, Jordan thought. They might as well enjoy what they could of it. Too bad he couldn't pull her to him for that kiss. He hadn't been kidding when he'd said he could use one...and a whole lot more.

Last night, he'd found himself in the middle of the very same dream he'd had after first meeting Tess Cameron. Once again, he'd wandered through that huge garden and discovered a welcoming woman waiting for him, arms outstretched and wearing only a yellow rose tucked behind one ear. Yet he still hadn't been able to make out all of her, even though he now knew how soft her skin felt under his palms. Nothing short of seeing the whole of her—and not just in dreams—would satisfy him.

Too damn bad he currently had to settle for a lot less, Jordan told himself.

But as much as a part of him would have liked to, he remained determined not to brood about that frustrating fact when the movie started minutes later after a Bugs Bunny cartoon. The opening credits were flashing on the screen to a lively tune as he followed up a handful of warm popcorn with a short swallow of cold cola and ventured another long glance in the rearview mirror. Glenda, he noted, still looked thoughtful. A lot more thoughtful than upset. The sight was enough to have him beginning to believe that the showdown in the diner might not have been such a bad thing, especially since no one had wound up on the wrong end of a fist. Or in handcuffs. At least her husband had clearly demonstrated that he cared more than enough to have the green-eyed monster gnawing at his gut.

Watching now as Frank casually placed an arm across the top of the dark leather seat and Glenda merely leaned back and settled in beside him, Jordan decided that things just might be headed in the right direction. Maybe. Hopefully.

Finally.

AS THE MOVIE WORE ON, Tess finished her popcorn and downed the last of her drink, thinking that even Travolta in his prime hadn't been able to stop her from endlessly speculating on how things were going in the back seat. All she knew for certain was that her parents had been peacefully—or ominously—quiet for some time.

For his part, Jordan seemed to be doing his best to keep his eyes on the huge screen while tossing occasional glances in the rearview mirror. Unfortunately, she didn't have that option, not unless she leaned over and craned her neck. Which would hardly be subtle, she told herself. She'd be better off tossing a look behind her if she wanted to satisfy her curiosity. She started to turn her head, then stilled completely as a soft voice slipping over her shoulder issued a throaty murmur.

"Ooh, Frank."

Still frozen in place, Tess slid a sidelong glance Jordan's way and found his gaze waiting to meet hers. For a hushed moment, they just stared at each other. Then another low yet far deeper voice rose from behind them.

"Mmm, baby."

Tess's eyes went wide as she came to a rapid conclusion. As far as she was concerned, those breathy murmurs could only mean that her parents were making out like a couple of teenagers! Whether that was wishful thinking or not, she wanted to laugh out loud just for the pure joy of it, and maybe punch a victorious hand in the air, as well. But most of all, she wanted to know exactly what was happening in the back seat.

"What's going on?" she asked, mouthing the words more than saying them as she kept her gaze on the man beside her.

Half-turned toward her, with one long arm resting

on the steering wheel, Jordan aimed another quick look in the rearview mirror. When *his* eyes widened, Tess felt the temperature take a hike that had nothing to do with the balmy night. Then his gaze again met hers, this time head-on, and everything else did a swift fade into the background.

Whatever her parents were doing, Tess thought, there was no doubt about what Jordan wanted to do, no mistaking the stark desire in his stare, no way she could deny that she wished they were the ones in the back seat making out for all they were worth. When he slid a hand over and laid it on her denim-clad knee, rubbing slowly, her pulse tripled. When she placed a hand on his knee in return, she didn't miss the sight of a broad chest rising as he sucked in a breath. Now they were both rubbing, and soon Tess had to look away. It was either that or throw herself straight into strong arms.

Her effort to slow things down, including her pulse, wasn't helped by the fact that the screen now showed the movie's stars engaging in a sexy bump-and-grind dance as the story headed to a close. Or that her own personal sexy man's fingers were suddenly moving up to her thigh, to rub and rub…

When closing credits were finally scrolling, Tess had to swallow hard to get a word out. "I think it's time to leave," she said, raising her voice to be sure everyone heard.

Jordan pulled his wandering hand to him and cleared his throat. "I'd say you're right." With that, he started the engine, revved it for a second, then pulled out.

Tess, having regained her own wayward hand, gathered up the empty popcorn and soda containers resting on the floor, which Jordan tossed in a trash bin as they left the drive-in. ‘‘Good movie,’’ she offered in a bid to make conversation.

‘‘Great,’’ Jordan replied shortly, keeping his eyes on the dark road as they drove down a winding two-lane highway leading back to Harmony proper. Silence reigned for most of the brief trip that ended when he pulled into his driveway.

Tess opened her door as the engine died, then hopped to the ground and turned in time to see her father helping her mother out. Both looked a little flushed, even in the dim glow cast by a nearby streetlight. Both also had the smallest, slyest smiles curving their lips.

Their daughter was wondering which bedroom they would choose to share that night when her father spoke at last, gazing straight at his wife. ‘‘I’m proposing—’’

Glenda stopped him in mid-word with a laugh coming from low in her throat. ‘‘I seem to remember your doing that a long time ago—on one knee, as a matter of fact.’’

Frank grinned. ‘‘What I’m proposing now is a wild weekend in Mexico.’’ He gave her a broad wink. ‘‘Are you game, baby?’’

‘‘Wild? *Now?*’’ His wife’s eyes went round, but only for a moment. Then she was nodding. ‘‘We could make it as far as Phoenix tonight. Maybe even, ah, find that motel that specialized in…’’ Her voice trailed off.

It was his turn to nod and lift a knowing brow. ‘‘Think it’s still there?’’

‘‘We can only hope,’’ she replied wryly, and laughed again.

After that, things happened quickly, with Glenda catching her daughter's hand and leading the way into the house so she could pack. Frank headed off in the opposite direction with Jordan to do the same. In a matter of minutes, Tess was hugging her parents goodbye on her front-porch steps. They'd be back on Monday to spend the night, they told her, and then they would start for San Diego Tuesday morning and take Ali with them.

"I plan to spend a lot of time the rest of the summer with both my gals," Frank said firmly.

Tess fixed him with a mock stern look. "See that you do," she said, and gave him another hug for good measure.

Then she was waving with one hand held high as they drove off in her father's Camaro, a bright-orange streak that rumbled its way rapidly down the street. If there had been some trailing streamers and a sign taped to the trunk saying Mexico Or Bust, she thought, it would have been perfect.

Conscious of what she wanted to do—had to do—next, Tess made a quick detour back into the house to make sure the cat would be okay for the night. Finding that plump ball of fur napping on her daughter's bed, she said, "I'll be home tomorrow, Roxy. And so will the one you like best." She hadn't forgotten her plan to pick up Ali midmorning at Mary Elizabeth's.

Roxy offered a loud purr at that last news as Tess left the room and headed down the stairs. She stopped only long enough to lock the front door. Then she all but ran to Jordan's place, and arrived on his doorstep just in time to have him opening the door to greet her with his own keys in hand, as if he'd had the very same idea. For a humming instant, they studied each other. Then Tess took a deep breath and told him something she'd been waiting for days to say.

"I'm still ready."

Chapter Eight

Jordan took Tess's keys from her hand, added them to his and tossed the whole bunch over his shoulder. They landed somewhere with a solid plop. Then he pulled her into the house, shut the door behind her and tugged her to him.

"I'm so ready I'm about to explode," he ground out, looking straight into her eyes as she stared up at him and meaning every husky word. If she hadn't come to him, he would have been knocking on her door right this minute. Or maybe banging on it would be more accurate. If he kissed her now, they'd wind up making love on the hall carpet. He was dead sure of that. So instead of lowering his head to hers, he caught her up in his arms and started for the stairs to the second floor.

"I wanted it to be slow the first time," he said as he tackled the steps in a rapid climb, "but I'm afraid it's not going to be like that, not now." He'd be lucky if he managed to keep her with him. No, whatever happened, he told himself, he had to make sure she was with him—all the way.

"Foreplay," he muttered under his breath. He had better remember that little detail.

"What did you say?" Tess asked, sounding breathless.

"Nothing." He deliberately kept his gaze straight ahead. He didn't trust certain parts of him enough to risk so much as a look, not until he got them both to his bed. Then he planned to look plenty.

"I guess you are in a hurry," she said as he all but raced through the bedroom doorway, his path marked by a wide shaft of light spilling in from the hall.

Slow it down, Trask, he told himself when he reached the brass double bed. He closed his eyes, tight, and carefully lowered the woman he held to her feet. Then he took a blind step back. Taking a long breath, he clenched his teeth and counted to ten in an effort to rein in his baser instincts.

"Jordan?" Tess ventured softly. The sound only served to remind him how soft and silky she was—probably all over—so he had to suck in another breath while he upped the count to twenty.

"Aren't you going to look at me?"

"In a minute."

"Is something wrong?"

"No. I just have to get a grip on myself."

She mulled that over for a second. "Why?"

He was past the point of being subtle. "Because I want to ravish you on the spot," he said bluntly.

"Oh." Stark silence followed before she spoke again. "I really think you should look at me."

Okay, he thought. Maybe he could do that now. Maybe.

So he looked, and then he had to stare, long and hard, as he took in the sight of Tess's wide, sultry smile. "Actually," she said, every bit as softly as before, "I've been giving some thought to ravishing you."

With that, she reached out, fisted one small hand in the much-washed fabric of his T-shirt and tugged him to her, with little trouble since the last thing he considered was resisting. He wasn't, after all, made of stone.

"Then again," she added, smiling that same siren's smile, "maybe we should ravish each other."

He locked his arms around her without hesitation. "Sounds like a plan to me."

The words were barely out when they hit the edge of the bed, and things happened quickly after that. Somehow he managed to get her out of her shirt in record time, and it took her scarce seconds to return the favor.

"I think your boots have to come off next," she told him, after pausing to stroke smooth fingers through the swirls of dark hair on his chest in a way that threatened to cloud his brain.

"Right. Boots."

He dealt with them and slipped off her sandals in the process, then angled her body full length on the bed. Perching himself on the lower half of the mattress, he ran his palms up denim-clad legs and over gently curved hips. With a will of its own, his mouth came down and headed straight for pert breasts covered by a plain white cotton bra.

There, he lingered. Rather than stripping the barrier away, as the more persistent parts of him urged, he tasted its treasures right through it, and was more than rewarded for his hard-won restraint when Tess suddenly writhed under him, clutched his head to her and issued a throaty moan.

"Ooh, Jordan."

And he found that all he could offer by way of a reply, when he finally lifted his head and nibbled his way to a creamy shoulder, was something that broke free from deep in his throat and surfaced with a craggy groan.

"Mmm, baby."

At that moment, his ego would have welcomed nothing more than another moan from the woman who smelled like buttered popcorn, floral soap and all female to him. Instead, he got a startled gasp quickly followed by a spurt of laughter. He was still trying to grasp the fact that her hips were no longer moving invitingly under his when she spoke.

"I, ah, think we have company."

His head shot up. "We have *what?*"

The lips he hadn't even gotten around to kissing yet curved wryly. "Company...of the canine variety."

Jordan slowly angled a look toward the side of the bed and found himself gazing straight into his faithful companion's unblinking stare. "Jeez," he managed to get out, and watched Jones greet the heartfelt statement with a lolling tongue and rapidly wagging tail, as if everything were just fine and dandy in the dog's world.

He drew in a steadying breath and levered himself up on his elbows, then dropped a glance down when the woman still lying mostly under him snorted out another laugh. "It's not that funny," he muttered.

She lifted a hand and lightly ran it through his hair. "Yes, it is. "You've just lost your sense of humor."

He couldn't argue on that score. "I'll be right back," he said, and reluctantly pushed himself away.

"Come on, pal," he added as he headed for the door to the hall. "I'm going to make your night."

Tess had to smile as she watched both males depart, wondering exactly what the dog's master had meant by that last comment. But her smile disappeared a second later as the stark reality of something hit and had her staring blankly into space.

She, Tess Cameron, a down-to-earth, everyday-average woman, was in Jordan Trask's bedroom, in that far-from-ordinary, larger-than-life man's bed. And not just to sleep.

With the way things had been happening so quickly, she and her nerves hadn't had time to consider that fact. Not until now.

It was ridiculous to be nervous, she told herself. Just a week earlier, she'd been more than eager to proceed full speed ahead. Then again, a week earlier she'd primped for hours for the main event and taken pains to dress for the occasion.

Tess bit her lower lip as she thought about taking off the rest of her clothes and hopping under the covers before a certain man returned. Then she thought about just getting under the covers, wearing her practical underwear and well-worn jeans. What she didn't want to think about was the undeniable truth that her lacy lingerie remained in a bottom dresser drawer, along with the more feminine of her nightgowns.

So what should she do?

The decision was made for her when Jordan jogged back through the door just then and shut it behind him. He crossed the room through the scant light filtering in through the curtained window and switched on the small lamp beside the bed. Narrowing her gaze in the golden glow that abruptly lit the room, Tess suddenly wished she had hopped under the covers while she'd had the chance, with or without her clothes.

But then he was grinning down at her, his good mood apparently restored, and her nerves fled in the face of that wonderfully wicked curve of firm lips.

"What did you do with your friend?" she asked, doing her best to return that grin with a small one of her own as he lowered himself to stretch out beside her.

"I let him sleep on the bed next door, when he usually has to settle for the rug in here. And I threw in a midnight snack of dog treats for good measure." Jordan tossed a long arm around her and pulled her closer. "When he polishes those off, he's welcome to chew on one of my silk ties that's still hanging from the headboard. Probably all it's fit for, anyway, after I had to use it to tie your father to the bedpost."

Tess blinked. "You did *what?*"

"It was in a good cause, trust me."

With that, he leaned in and touched his forehead to hers. "Now, where was I? Ah, yes. I remember."

And he did, as Tess soon discovered when his mouth beat a swift path to her breasts. He had her writhing again in minutes, had her clothes off before much longer, and all but growled his approval when she quickly undressed him. He took time out to reach into the nightstand drawer for a foil packet and deal with protection before he stretched the whole long length of himself over her and looked straight into her eyes.

"I don't know how slow I can go," he said, his voice rougher now, deeper, and male to the core.

"I think I can keep up," Tess replied. She had to hope so, at least, because she had no doubts about the fact that he was beyond waiting too long. Whatever happened, she told herself not to expect fireworks. For her, she couldn't help recalling, sex had always been pleasant yet hardly spectacular.

But she hadn't counted on this particular man's ability to make her feel what she had never felt before, take her somewhere she had never been before. And quickly. Scarce seconds after he'd slipped inside her with one long stroke and established a pulse-pounding rhythm, she found herself on the brink of beginning an astonishing journey.

"Are you with me?" he asked wondrous minutes later, gritting out the words as his breath started to come hard and fast.

"Yes," she said on a gasp. And fully meant it.

Her last coherent thought before everything in her swiftly soared to the heights in a glorious burst of pure pleasure, before Jordan's hoarse shout rang out to mingle with her quiet cry, was that fireworks had turned out to be far from beyond her. All she'd needed was a larger-than-life man to light the fuse.

THEY FINALLY FELL into an exhausted sleep, after another bout of lovemaking almost as frantic as the first, and Tess woke up with a smile on her face just as the sky began to lighten with the bare beginnings of dawn. She might have slept longer, she knew, if she'd been alone. Sharing a bed again would take some getting used to, she decided with a small yawn.

Not that she had any complaints about the night just past. And certainly no regrets. As a lover, Jordan had more than fulfilled her expectations.

He might take up a great deal of the bed, forcing her to snuggle next to him for all she was worth to keep from falling off, but snuggling up to a hard, hair-roughened body so unlike her own definitely had its rewards. Listening to the earliest of the birds chirping in the trees and humming softly along with them while a long wall of solid male warmed her back was another plus. A big one.

"Do you usually hum before the sun comes up?" a low voice asked at her ear.

Once again, her smile broke through as she wiggled toes covered by a powder-blue sheet. "Only when I'm happy."

Warm lips dropped a kiss on a bare shoulder. "Then I take it that I managed to, ah, fill the bill last night."

There was too much macho-male satisfaction in that short statement to let her believe he had any doubts on that score. She tucked her tongue in her cheek. "Let's just say you basically did a good job."

He rolled her over in one smooth motion, until she lay flat on her back, then stared down at her, actually looking insulted. "*Good.*"

She had to laugh. "Okay, maybe it was spectacular."

"Humph. That's more like it."

Lifting a hand, she stroked one finger over the dark stubble on a chiseled jaw. "How did you sleep?"

"Great—" he fixed her with a mock frown "—until the humming started."

Not at all repentant, she released a deliberately exaggerated sigh. "You know, I'm detecting a pattern here. This is twice I've seen you up with the birds, and both times you've been grumpy."

"I'm never grumpy," he declared soundly. But his lips twitched before he pursed them. "Must be your imagination."

"Mmm. How about grouchy?"

He growled and got even by giving her a quick tickle under the sheet that had her laughing again.

"As for myself," she told him when she regained her breath, "I love the mornings. Even as a teenager, I never wanted to laze away the day." She tilted her head. "Were you one of those teens some desperate parents have to haul out of bed?"

He hesitated, and this time the slight frown that formed on a lightly tanned forehead looked far more genuine. When a soft scratching sound suddenly started on the bedroom door, he aimed a rapid glance in that direction and let out a short breath. "I think we have company again."

Within seconds he was on his feet and pulling on a pair of dark briefs. "Jones probably wants to do his duty. I'll let him out and be right back."

With that, Jordan opened the door to the tune of a happy canine yelp and quickly closed it behind him, leaving the woman in his bed to form her own thoughtful frown. Would he have talked about his teenage years if they hadn't been interrupted? Tess asked herself, punching up a pillow and leaning against it. Somehow she didn't think so. It certainly hadn't escaped her notice how adept he seemed to be at avoiding any real discussion of his past. During all the time they'd spent together, he had never brought up the subject, and when she had, he'd smoothly skirted around it.

That shouldn't bother her, reason said. The man was entitled to his privacy. But, even though she firmly believed in everyone's right to choose to keep things private, she had to admit that it did bother her in this particular case. More so, she couldn't deny, now that they had spent the night together.

Caught up in her thoughts, Tess was still frowning into space when the door opened. But no frown could hold out against the unexpected sight of Jordan standing in the doorway still dressed in his briefs and clutching a small yellow rose in one large hand. It could only have come from her garden, and that conclusion had her slowly arching a brow.

''Did you scale the fence to pick that flower?''

He flashed her a grin. ''Guilty as charged.''

''Wearing just your underwear?''

''It's warm outside.'' He closed the door behind him with a soft click. ''And no one was up yet to see me except the birds.''

He walked toward her then, moving with a simple masculine grace that she had to admire. Heck, she had to admire every gorgeous inch. ''How come you chose the rose?'' she asked.

''I'm about to fulfill a fantasy,'' Jordan told her. ''That is...if you'll cooperate.'' *And I'm hoping, badly, that you will.* He watched and waited then, saw both of Tess's brows take a sharp climb as his quiet words hit home, caught the wary look that gradually entered her gaze.

''What, um, did you have in mind?''

He had to swallow a chuckle. ''Nothing that involves your being tied to the bedpost, I promise.''

Bending over, he whispered some quietly specific words in her ear and eventually had her nodding in agreement. Then he carefully tucked the small rosebud he held behind that very same ear, took a long step back, and again watched and waited as she brushed the sheet aside and slowly rose to stand in front of him.

When she lifted her arms and held them out in welcome, he decided it was indeed his dream come true. No, even better, much better, because he could make out all of her in the pink-tinged light of a brand-new day. Tess Cameron wasn't the most beautiful woman he'd ever met. He knew that full well. But the picture she presented right now was the most beautiful sight he'd ever seen, no contest. Somehow that seemed to make perfect sense.

Not that he'd be content just looking. This time, though, he planned to take things slow. Keeping that firmly in mind, he closed the short distance between them and reached for her. In the next moment her arms closed around him, and it felt as if he'd found what he'd been searching for, just as in his dream.

"What else does this fantasy involve?" she asked, nuzzling her nose in the crook of his neck.

Satisfaction was still rolling through him. "From here on, I'll have to make it up as we go along."

And he began to do precisely that, first kissing her until they both had to struggle for air, then finally allowing himself to touch at will, and at length. Gently, thoroughly, skillfully, he stroked his fingers down her, over her...into her. And caught her around the waist when her knees buckled.

He sent her over then, relishing her response even as his mouth drank in her cry of release. "I think it's time to try the bed," he murmured at last, holding her through the aftershocks.

"Yes," Tess gasped out, still clinging to him.

After grabbing up protection and getting them both

stretched out on the tangled sheets, he wasted no time in saying, ''I'm trying for more than spectacular this round.''

Blue eyes met hazel. ''How about...incredible?''

He ran his hands down her again. ''Yeah, I like that one.''

And he got what he wanted endless minutes later, after he'd held back as long as he could and had to surge inside, had to give pleasure even as he received it in return, had to satisfy building needs he could no longer control. The last thing he heard before his body revved for a final plunge was Tess's breathless whisper as she shuddered again in his arms.

''Incredible.''

TESS WAS STILL CONSIDERING just how incredible the events in a certain man's bedroom had been much later that day when her daughter's voice returned her to far different surroundings.

''I think Mr. T's pretty cool, Mom.''

Tess couldn't smother a small smile. ''I guess I do, too. He's a...good neighbor.'' Which, she thought, was true enough, even if last night he had become so much more—to her.

Ali propped her elbows on a red-and-white checkered tablecloth. ''Is that why he took us out for pizza?''

''Something like that,'' Tess hedged. The total truth there was that he'd simply invited himself along when she'd mentioned a plan to treat Ali to dinner at her favorite restaurant before her grandparents took her back to California. As a thank-you for letting Ali spend the night, Tess had asked Mary Elizabeth's mother if the bubbly young girl with impish green eyes and a mass of short golden curls could join them.

"I think he's dreamy," the little blonde said from her place at the square oak table.

People were sometimes surprised, Tess knew, that the two girls were such good friends, since they seemed as opposite as night and day. Where Ali favored plain overalls and jeans, Mary was partial to bright pants and tops. Where Mary idolized the latest preteen TV stars, Ali only considered railroad veterans worthy of that honor. And the list went on and on.

"Yuck." Ali made a face and shook her head, sending brown braids swaying. "*Dreamy?* Come on, Mary E, gimme a break."

Mary Elizabeth lifted a small chin and pursed bow-shaped lips that were several shades lighter than her hot-pink outfit. "Well then, he's a hunk."

Ali rolled her eyes. "He's a grown-up, that's what he is." She blew out a short, exasperated breath. "Mr. T is *way* older than the two of us put together."

"Maybe I should have brought my cane," Jordan said dryly as he suddenly stood beside the table, a plastic tray holding four frosted tumblers in hand.

Smothering the urge to laugh, Tess glanced up at him. "Oh, I don't think you need it." She waited a beat. "Yet."

"Thanks. I feel better now."

The girls shared a giggle as drinks were passed around, and Jordan told his companions the pizzas would be ready shortly. "I ordered a couple with the works. I can only hope my *way*-old stomach will be able to handle it."

Ali giggled again. "You're teasing, aren't you?"

Jordan nodded. "Yeah, you figured it out."

"That's because I'm smart," the girl told him. Rather than a boast, it was a simple statement of fact.

"We're both smart," Mary Elizabeth chimed in.

He looked from one of them to the other. "I don't doubt that for a minute," he said, and watched twin toothy grins form. "There's some artistic talent at the table, too," he added, aiming his gaze at Ali. "I like the train pictures on your refrigerator."

"I did them all by myself," she replied with more than a hint of pride. "Mary E's brother taught me. Robbie's gonna take art stuff in college when he finishes high school."

"Ohmigosh." Mary Elizabeth's eyes had gone wide. "I forgot to tell you about the drawing contest at Harmony Park, Al. It's on Monday morning, and it's for all the kids in town, big and little. Everyone has to draw something in the park, and they get a prize if they win. Me and Robbie are going. My mom's gonna drop us off there on her way to work at the bank, and take us back home on her lunch hour."

Ali's eyes all but glowed with enthusiasm as she turned to Tess. "Oh, Mom. Can I go with them?"

"Robbie will watch us both at the park," Mary Elizabeth offered on her older brother's behalf.

Which was the very reason for her personal reluctance to agree, Tess had to admit. The teenager had acted as baby-sitter for Ali at home before, and they got along well. That was no problem. But keeping track of two lively girls in the middle of what was bound to be a crowd could be asking a bit too much of a fifteen-year-old who'd be participating in the contest himself.

She said exactly that, as diplomatically as possible, and added, "You were going to go to work with me, honey, remember?"

Ali sat back, the light in her eyes fading. "I know, but I could win a prize, Mom." She hesitated. "Do you have to go to work on Monday?"

"Yes."

There was nothing else she could say, and Tess told herself not to feel guilty about disappointing her child. As a working mother, she'd known for some time that choices had to be made. This time, she had to choose to do her job. New landscaping was scheduled to go in on the grounds of the main library, and muscle provided by several college boys looking to earn some extra money had already been lined up. In an emergency, she wouldn't have hesitated a bare instant to put her daughter first. This, however, was no emergency.

"Okay." Ali accepted the reality of the situation with a resigned sigh. But she still looked forlorn.

"Why don't you two girls go up to the counter and check on the pizzas," Jordan suggested.

With the resiliency of youth, Ali readily fell in with that plan. The girls were barely gone, leaving hand in hand, when the man seated at her left switched his gaze to Tess. "You know, I could go along to keep an eye on things at the park and drop Ali off where you're working when the big event is over."

Startled, she straightened in her seat and just stared for a second. "Do you want to do that?"

He shrugged. "I wouldn't mind."

"Really?"

"Really." His smile broke through then, and despite the hubbub going on all around them in the popular restaurant, it had her pulse fluttering. ''Don't worry, Tess,'' he said. ''I'll take good care of her.''

''I know.'' And she did. Knew, in fact, that this man might well have already risked his own well-being to keep others safe. ''Nevertheless,'' she felt compelled to add, ''I don't want to impose on you.''

''You're hardly doing that,'' he pointed out mildly, leaning back in his chair. ''I'm offering. And, when you come right down to it, how much trouble can it be?''

HOW MUCH TROUBLE CAN IT BE? The memory of those words was already coming back to haunt Jordan when he finally found an open space in the crowded, tree-shaded lot at Harmony Park and watched Ali and his two other passengers eagerly jump out. Maybe, Jordan thought, he should have let the other kids be dropped off by their mother, as was originally planned before he'd volunteered to take them all. Before he'd known what he was letting himself in for. Before he'd been treated to a dose of parenthood.

But then the woman trying to get to work would have been treated to two return trips to her sprawling, ranch-style house—after being halfway to the park both times—to retrieve desperately needed items that had somehow been left behind. Either that, or she would have made dead sure her offspring had absolutely everything required before they started out.

Probably the latter, he had to admit in hindsight. Not that there was any way he could have predicted that the prospect of doing without a particular shade of drawing chalk out of a nearly full box would be a tearful event to a little blonde, or that her reed-slim, red-haired brother, who seemed to favor T-shirts touting the world of modern art, would run out the door mistakenly carrying a filled-to-the-max sketching pad slung under a long arm, rather than the new one purchased for the occasion.

Jordan supposed he had to be downright grateful that the third crisis to abruptly rear its head had only meant a short detour to the nearest grocery for a pack of chewing gum, which had turned out to be a vital part of Ali's drawing routine. If her jaws weren't moving, the creative juices just didn't flow. Apparently.

God bless mothers everywhere who dealt with this kind of thing every day, Jordan thought with an inner sigh as he followed the trio of young artists down a winding sidewalk lined with flowering bushes that led to an open area where a group of brightly decorated folding tables had been set up for the festivities. Balloons, he noted, had been used to maximum advantage, swaying in the light, warm wind.

All at once, Ali stopped in her tracks and whipped around on well-worn running shoes. "Oh, Mr. T, I forgot—"

Jordan halted her with an upraised palm. Enough, he decided, was enough. "Whatever it is, you'll just have to do without it," he said. And meant it.

She shook her head. "It's not an *it.* I just forgot to tell you that Mrs. Fontinella—she was my teacher last year—called this morning while my mom was in the shower. She wanted to know if Mom was coming to the contest, 'cause one of the judges couldn't and they needed another one, and I..."

"And you said your mother wasn't coming," Jordan helpfully supplied at the hesitation, wondering why his instincts were urging him to turn around and take off. Now.

Ali smiled a sunny smile that only served to make the back of his neck tingle. ''Miss Fontinella was real sorry that my mom couldn't be a judge,'' the girl confided. ''But I made her feel better when I said I thought you could do it.''

He could do it? With three pairs of eyes now studying him, Jordan knew he had to come up with a good reason why he couldn't, and fast. Thankfully, it didn't take him long to produce one. ''Judges have to be impartial,'' he declared. ''It wouldn't be right for me to be a part of a contest any of you are in.''

Ali's smile didn't falter. ''That's what Mrs. Fontinella said, so she decided you could judge the little kids.''

He lifted a wary brow. ''Little?''

''Yep.'' Ali nodded briskly. ''You're gonna have fun, Mr. T. Those guys in kindergarten can draw pretty good.''

TESS WAS DIRECTING the planting of a small cluster of baby pines when Jordan's black Explorer came up the circular driveway leading to the two-story redbrick library trimmed in snowy white. It had barely stopped at the curb when Ali hopped out and ran over with a large sheet of paper flapping in one hand.

''Mom, I took second place in my group!''

Tess grabbed her up for a hearty hug. ''That's wonderful, honey. Let me see what you did.'' She discovered the crayon drawing featured a quartet of brown ducks waddling in lush green grass with the park's ivory marble fountain in the background.

''Obviously a masterpiece,'' a low voice remarked

as Tess studied her daughter's effort. She glanced up, met Jordan's gaze, and had to wonder if her eyes were deceiving her or if he really did look a little... frazzled. Certainly there was no denying that his glossy dark hair was intriguingly mussed, as though he'd recently raked his fingers through it more than once.

"Indeed a small masterpiece," she said, and returned her gaze to her daughter. "You did a fine job, pumpkin."

"And I won a cool pen." Ali pulled it from an overall pocket to let the sun high overhead sparkle on its shiny chrome surface. "Grandma and Grandpa are gonna be surprised when they get back tonight." Tess didn't hesitate to agree, and the girl returned her new treasure to its resting place, then glanced around. "You planted a lot of stuff today."

"I had a lot of help." Tess brushed a thin line of rich, black dirt off her khaki uniform pants and aimed a grateful grin at the well-muscled college kids who had worked hard all morning. More than a few returned it with quick grins of their own, and one undeniably bad-boy type followed his up with a slow wink that might have had her sighing in response—if she were sixteen.

Ali greeted them all with a wave and ran over to show off her prize-winning picture. Soon many of the young men, mostly dressed in sleeveless T-shirts and denim cutoffs, were bent over the effort, with one little girl chatting a mile a minute.

"I could have helped," Jordan said.

There was the barest edge of something in his voice, something that had Tess suspecting he'd caught that bad-boy wink and didn't appreciate the sight. She turned her head to find him now standing only inches away. "You did help, a lot, by keeping tabs on Ali. I have to thank you."

He gazed down at her for a long moment, then dipped his head and said, "I'll accept your thanks…and this." Before she knew it, firm lips had settled on hers.

He didn't kiss her long, or hard. Just hard enough and long enough to have her blood zinging in her veins. Then he pulled back, waved a casual goodbye to their abruptly rapt audience—including an all-eyes Ali—and started for the curb with a pointed wink of his own directed squarely at Tess that she could only blink at.

Taking in a steadying breath, she watched him drive away with quick efficiency as Ali came running to stand beside her. "Mr. T kissed you, Mom."

At that moment, all Tess could come up with in response was, "Yes, well, ah, he's definitely a good neighbor."

THE FOLLOWING MORNING Jordan was still far from regretting the impulse that had led to kissing Tess in front of the library. After all, he thought as he stacked breakfast dishes to dry, it was the only real physical contact they'd had since she'd left his bed early on Saturday. Not that he had anticipated things being any different. Tess Cameron was hardly the sort to conduct an affair with a young and impressionable daughter close by. He would never have expected it of her, but that didn't ease the need to have her under him again. And he wanted more than that, he knew. He wanted to be with her—in and out of bed.

Last night, he would have settled for dinner, with

her and the whole group staying at her house. He'd seen her parents pull into her driveway, tooting the Camaro's horn in greeting, late in the afternoon through his living room window. But he hadn't been invited over, hadn't really thought he would be. As far as he was concerned, Tess had every right to spend some time alone with her daughter and parents before they left to head back to California, and every right not to invite him to join them.

He wasn't a part of the family.

Jordan wouldn't argue that point for a second. And the last thing he'd let himself do was start brooding over the fact that he'd eaten a solitary meal at a local restaurant. No way.

Just forget the whole thing, Trask, he flat out ordered, and found that silent statement underscored in the next breath by the merry chime of the front door bell.

Seconds later, he discovered Frank Fitzgerald and Ali Cameron waiting on his doorstep. "Thought we'd pop over and say goodbye before we got on the road," Frank told him.

"Come on in," he said. "There's still some coffee left."

Frank declined with a quick shake of his head as they walked in. "I've already had plenty, thanks."

Ali looked up at Jordan. "Can I say goodbye to Jones, too, while we're here?"

"Sure. He's in the backyard right now. You know the way out through the kitchen."

"Yep." With that, she was off at a run, and the two men were left standing in the hall.

"We could sit down," Jordan suggested, fighting back a yawn. There'd been nothing to disturb his sleep the night before, but he still hadn't managed to get much of it. After only one night with Tess at his side, his bed had seemed far too empty.

"I'll just be staying a minute." Frank rocked back on his heels and shoved his hands into the pockets of the jeans he'd been talked into buying. "I want to thank you, Trask—for everything. I'm not much with words, not when I need them, but I've got to tell you that I damn well appreciate what you did. And I know Glenda would the say the same, only better than I can."

Jordan's lips curved at the corners. "You're welcome, for whatever I managed to do. I hope you have a good trip back."

"I plan on it." Suddenly Frank's expression sobered as a frown formed. "You know, once Glenda and I started talking, she told me a few things about what she saw—or maybe what she figured she just missed—when she got here."

Okay. Here it comes, Jordan thought. Deciding to meet it head-on, he shoved both hands into the back pockets of his Levi's, widened his stance on the hall carpet, and didn't let his gaze waver as he stared straight into Frank's laser blues.

"And what I suppose I have to say now," the older man went on, "is that Tess is still my girl—she always will be—and I wouldn't look kindly on any man who tried to take advantage of her—although she'd probably want my hide for interfering."

Silence hung heavy in the air between them before Jordan spoke, his voice soft yet edged with steel. "I've never taken advantage of any woman. I'm not that kind of man, Fitzgerald."

Frank nodded slowly. "No, I didn't think you

were.'' All at once, a brief grin flashed across a broad face. ''But that doesn't mean I wouldn't come back and do my best to pound you into the ground, ace, if it turns out I was wrong.''

Jordan had to grin himself. ''Fair enough.''

Frank extended an arm for a firm handshake. ''Take care, Trask. I'll start loading up while you say goodbye to my freckle-faced angel. I'll be a while, so don't hurry.'' He blew out a breath. ''Glenda went crazy and bought a ton of pottery in Nogales. After a few tequilas, I just egged her on, so now we've got cartons of the stuff to take back.''

After Frank left, grumbling good-naturedly about the pitfalls of wild weekends, Jordan found Ali sitting on the back-porch steps and leaning over to pet the basset hound basking in her attention. Jordan hunkered down and sat beside her, planting his boots on the concrete walkway at the foot of the stairs and propping his forearms on his knees.

Ali angled a sidelong glance his way. ''I'm gonna miss Jones,'' she told him. ''And you, too, Mr. T.''

Before he could reply, she took a short breath and continued with a quick question that was issued far too casually. ''Did you like kissing my mom?''

Uh-oh, Jordan thought. He probably should have seen that one coming. ''Yeah,'' was all he could say, because he wouldn't lie about it.

''Hmm.'' Ali suddenly bore a distinct resemblance to her grandmother as she mulled things over. ''I guess that's good,'' she said at last, '''cause I think my mom liked it, too.'' She took another second to study him. ''And it's okay with me, I mean, if you both want to do it again.''

An eight-year-old was giving him permission to

court her mother. Jordan couldn't take it any other way. He wasn't exactly sure how he felt about it, but it had a smile tugging at his lips, anyway. "I suppose we just might want to do it again."

Ali dipped her head in a slow and seemingly satisfied nod, as though, to her, the whole thing were settled. Then she reached a small hand up to lightly brush a finger over one side of his jaw. "You got a cut, right here."

He lifted a shoulder in a slight shrug. "Just a nick from shaving. You're lucky you're never going to have to deal with a big, bad morning beard."

She giggled, as he expected, but there was no way he could have anticipated what happened next when she craned her neck as far it would go and pressed soft little lips to his jaw. It was the first time in his memory that anyone had tried to ease his wounds with a kiss. Right now, it made him feel like a king.

"Is that better?" she asked.

He had to clear his throat. "A whole lot."

"I hope your plant gets better, too," she told him, gazing past him to the side of the steps. As even as her tone was, the suddenly solemn cast of dark eyes said she had grave doubts about that particular outcome.

"It's going to make it," Jordan didn't hesitate to firmly reply. At least it still didn't seem to be in any worse shape than it had on the day he'd brought it home, he thought to himself as he studied the object in question. Or maybe it did, he had to concede. But only a little. It was hanging in there, at any rate.

Ali gave Jones a last pat and stood up. "I gotta go. Grandpa says we have to make tracks this morning."

She was turning to start back up the steps when

Jordan offered an alternative. ‘‘I’ll give you a lift over the back fence,’’ he said, rising, ‘‘and save some time.’’

Seconds later, he caught her under the arms and raised her high, then angled her body past the fence, bent, and carefully dropped her to the grass on the other side. She landed with a laugh and looked up at him. ‘‘Thanks, Mr. T. I hope you have a way-cool summer.’’

Then she was gone with a jaunty wave, and Jordan could only gaze after her and shake his head at his own foolishness—because he knew without a doubt what had just happened.

It might not be smart, not if he wanted to play it safe and keep some emotional distance. But he’d gone and done it, anyway.

Wise or not, he’d fallen flat on his butt for one freckle-nosed, tomboy angel.

Chapter Nine

"Okay, I've told you all about the joys of taking a Florida vacation with a golf-nut husband and two theme-park-crazed kids." Sally sat forward and picked up her mug. "It's your turn to fill me in on what's been happening in your life."

Tess drummed a finger on the kitchen table, thinking it was hard to believe that only a few weeks had passed since the two of them were in this very same spot on another late Saturday morning discussing the merits of her doing something she had since—sometimes still amazingly to her—managed to accomplish.

"Well, let's see," she said, ticking off a mental list. "My parents had a brief marital crisis, which has thankfully been resolved. My daughter phoned yesterday to tell me she's going to Sea World this weekend with both of her grandparents in tow. We got the new landscaping at the library finished, and it looks terrific, if I do say so myself." She deliberately paused at that point and summoned the most offhand tone she could muster. "Oh, and I took a lover."

Sally choked on a swallow of coffee and set her mug down with a clatter, somehow avoiding spilling anything on the table or her cinnamon-colored tank top. "Holy Toledo!" she got out at last, a slyly pleased gleam rapidly sparking to life in her eyes. "I don't have to ask who it is, do I?"

"No, I don't suppose you do," Tess replied mildly.

"Jordan Trask," Sally summed up with confidence. "Boy, when I miss something, I really miss *something.*"

Tess swallowed a laugh. "Are you saying I should have waited until you got back?"

"I guess not," Sally conceded after giving it some consideration.

"Thanks," Tess said dryly.

"Still," Sally continued, ignoring the sarcasm, "I think I deserve a few details. For starters, did you jump him or did the gorgeous man jump you?"

"Let's just say we each discovered the other was ready to jump at nearly the same time." Which, Tess thought, seemed to sum things up fairly well.

Sally picked up her mug again. "So, how is he in that, um, area—" she arched a suggestive eyebrow "—I mean, on a scale of one to ten?"

"A hundred and twenty."

Eyes widening, Sally blew out a shimmering breath. "Whew. I'd ask for more data—beg for it, in fact—but I'm not sure my system can handle it."

Tess grinned. "I'm not about to give you a blow-by-blow description, anyway."

Sally leaned back in her chair and conducted a short study. "You're happy," she said in conclusion. "That's good to see."

"I am," Tess readily agreed. In fact, if someone had contended she was positively glowing at the moment, she wouldn't have doubted it for an instant. "Taking a lover definitely has its benefits."

"Mmm-hmm. I can tell." A thoughtful expression formed on the face of the woman Tess had known since they'd made mud pies—and a delightful mess—together as toddlers. "Maybe," Sally ventured after a long moment, "this will turn out to be more than an affair."

"No, it won't," Tess countered candidly. "It will be over when the summer's over."

Sally's dark brows drew together. "Has he said as much?"

Tess shook her head. "He didn't have to. There's never been any question in my mind that Jordan rented a place for the summer to give himself time to decide what to do next with his life. Once that happens, once he knows where he's headed, he'll leave Harmony...for good."

If she'd ever so much as considered doubting that outcome, Tess thought, the way he avoided discussing his past would have only served to remind her of the fact that he'd chosen to keep their relationship on a mainly physical level—which, she had to admit, probably went hand in glove with a temporary affair. Never having indulged in one before, she wasn't all that sure of the finer points involved, but throwing up a few roadblocks on the path to real intimacy seemed a safer route to take.

Trouble was, she couldn't completely stifle her curiosity, not when it came to the man who had shared a shower with her that morning before leaving to run some errands with his faithful dog tagging along. He and Jones were now spending the nights at her place more often than not, and only the plump cat considering herself to be the house's rightful owner took exception to their presence. In fact, Roxy went out of her way to turn her little nose up at her canine visitor every chance she got, while Jones had become very good at ignoring her attempts to take him down a peg. Tess could only wish she'd been half as successful at ignoring her nagging curiosity about the dog's owner and the life he'd led before coming to Harmony, but so far she hadn't had much luck in that effort.

"Could be you're right and Jordan will leave," Sally acknowledged, pulling Tess back to the conversation. "Then again, if he's looking as happy as you are these days, he just may decide to stay—especially if someone, ah, gave him a nudge in that direction."

"Uh-uh." Tess slid down in her chair and crossed her arms over the front of her white T-shirt. "I'm not nudging," she said, narrowing her gaze, "and neither are you."

Sally grimaced ruefully. "Oh, all right, I'll keep my two cents out of it. But that doesn't mean you have to."

"Yes, it does," Tess replied firmly, even as memories of another man, another relationship, slipped into her mind. "Believe me, the last thing a wise woman will do is try to hold on to a man who wants to leave."

A silent beat followed that statement before Sally said, "I have the feeling I just heard the voice of experience speaking." She paused, her expression sobering. "I know it's none of my business, but I can't help thinking you were referring to Roger."

Which, Tess told herself, was absolutely true. And maybe it was time to share a few hard truths about something she had never discussed with anyone other than her parents—and only with them when things had gotten to the point where she'd had no other choice, when she'd finally accepted the inevitable and had to prepare them for it. Maybe, she concluded in hindsight, it would have done her good to confide in Sally long ago. Certainly, if there was one person her own age she could talk to and trust to keep things private between them, it was the woman seated across from her.

"You're right," she said on a quiet sigh. "I was referring to Roger. And, unfortunately, to a marriage that was in trouble by the time we celebrated our second anniversary."

Rather than appear surprised in the least, Sally nodded slowly. "I'll admit I suspected things weren't what they should be early on and as time passed, the two of you just seemed to gradually grow more...distant. That's the only word I can come up with."

"Distant," Tess repeated thoughtfully. "That could describe it in a nutshell, I suppose. We did drift apart, slowly but surely after the first couple of years, although I can't deny that for a long time I did my best to pretend it wasn't happening, that Roger was as content as I was to be half of a comfortably married couple who'd settled down in a place many people would contend was an ideal spot to raise a family."

She sighed again, this time inwardly, remembering the young wife she'd been, the hopes for the future she'd stubbornly clung to. Desperately. Uselessly. "Then one day I couldn't pretend any longer, not when Roger suggested outright that we go our separate ways and I had to come to terms with how he felt, because there was no alternative. Roger loved Ali, he truly did, and he was a good father. I would never say otherwise. But he was tired of working as a computer tech at the power company here when he could be earning a better salary in a bigger city—tired of 'living life in the slow lane,' as he put it. And, although he never said so exactly, it was clear that he was tired of being a husband, as well.''

''Oh, Tess.''

''It's the truth, Sal, I'm afraid. Looking back, I can see that we never should have gotten married when we did. Not long after we met in college and things got serious, I knew I was ready to settle down, but Roger only thought he was until he found himself tied to the role of husband—and soon after that, father. As time passed, his growing discontent with being bound to a certain lifestyle began to chip away at our relationship. Instead of facing the truth, though, I deliberately disregarded the signs and hung on as long as I could to a man I should have known full well would only be content with leaving so he could find out what he'd missed by marrying too soon.'' She paused, drew in a breath. ''Which, as it turned out, never happened. We were still working the details out between us, how we would tell everyone, especially Ali, and handle joint custody, when Roger died without ever getting the chance to try life in a faster lane. Just like that, he was gone.''

Determined not to shed more tears—she'd already cried her share, and then some—Tess got up, mug in hand, and walked over to the coffeemaker on the counter to pour herself a refill. She took her time, took a last moment to consider her failed marriage, and finally let the memories go.

''I'm sorry,'' Sally said quietly and simply as Tess resumed her seat.

"I am, too, and thanks for listening."

"You're welcome."

Tess tried out a small smile and found it felt good. "Whatever happened then, I am happy now," she said, and could only be grateful it was the sheer truth.

"You've made a believer out of me," Sally told her frankly. "As I said before, it's good to see. And now I'm even more of the opinion that you deserve every bit of it."

"Spoken like a true friend."

"You got it."

"Still," Tess said, "the fact that I'm well pleased with the way recent events have turned out doesn't mean I plan on forgetting a hard lesson learned. No matter what, the last thing I'll ever do is cling to another man who wants to leave."

Sally ventured a soft smile of her own. "Could be this one won't want to."

"He will," Tess replied with assurance, certain she was right. She wasn't kidding anyone, most especially herself, about that. "Jordan isn't the type of man who'd be content to live here on a permanent basis. I've known that from the day we met. But—" she launched another and meaningfully wider smile "—I intend to enjoy him while he's here."

"I see." Sally leaned back and tapped a scarlet-tipped finger to her lips. "A hundred and twenty, huh?"

"Eat your heart out, Sal."

WAR HAD NO DOUBT BEEN inevitable, Jordan told himself as he headed up the stairs to the second floor a few nights later, his bare feet treading silently on the steps. Battles of the sexes had been waged for ages, probably going back to the time the first caveman couple, or maybe the first dinosaur duo, had locked horns over something or other, and the latest skirmish to take place on that front had been brewing for a while. When a haughty female continually lorded it over a lowly male, sooner or later something was bound to get ruffled.

In this case, it was fur.

And, naturally, the earsplitting clash had broken out at close to midnight, just when the house was at its most quiet. Wars had never been known to be convenient. He and Tess had been sound asleep, arms wrapped around each other and legs tangled. Which was usually the case these days, Jordan thought with an undeniably pleased curve of his lips. The fact that she readily welcomed him into her bed on a regular basis filled him with satisfaction, even made him want to beat his chest a little. *Yeah, Trask, just like Mr. Caveman.*

He merely shrugged at the inner voice mocking him, because he couldn't deny it and, besides, he felt too damn good to argue with anyone, himself included. His only regret at the moment was that he'd had to leave the considerable comforts of Tess's bed in the middle of the night to make peace. Still, the need for it wasn't all that surprising.

Jordan supposed a guy could only take so much, even if the guy in question was a dog.

"Everything okay?" Tess asked when he walked into the bedroom and closed the door.

Lying stretched out under a floral-print sheet, the top edge flirting with the swell of her breasts, she looked heavy eyed and temptingly mussed in the light of the small lamp by the bed. Certain parts of him stirred at the sight, parts that should have been a lot less eager after their earlier lovemaking.

"It is now," he told her as he flipped back the sheet and crawled in beside her. It occurred to him that it seemed as natural as if he'd been doing it for years. More natural, maybe, than it had seemed with any other woman. One thing he was dead certain of was that he didn't want any other woman. Right now, this woman suited him down to his toes.

It also occurred to him that he was more drawn to her, felt more for her, than he had ever felt for any woman. There seemed to be no question on that score, either. Not that he hadn't had his share of dealings with the opposite sex. He had. Not as many as some might think, because bed hopping had never held any great appeal for him, but his fair share, nonetheless. As pleasurable as the best of those relationships had been, though, he hadn't found himself fantasizing about them. It had taken Tess Cameron, backed by an army of flowers, to invade his dreams. That, he supposed, said a lot.

"What happened?" his dream woman asked, snuggling closer, just as he liked.

He turned and tangled his hair-roughened legs with her far softer ones. That was just the way he liked it, too. "Your cat apparently decided to try her luck at snatching the dog dish you bought for Jones."

"Uh-oh."

"Exactly."

"No wonder he brought the house down."

Jordan nodded. "The barking had mostly stopped and they were down to growling at each other by the time I got to the kitchen and broke things up."

Tess sighed, hard enough for her breath to flutter

over his neck. ''Well, I'm glad Jones stood up for himself.''

''Have to admit I feel the same way.'' Jordan ran a hand down a silky back, debating what the chances were of talking his bed partner into some physical activity before they gave sleep another try.

''He's entitled to what belongs to him,'' Tess declared, her mind still clearly on the confrontation, ''and Roxy's got to learn that everything isn't hers by right.''

''I'd say you have a point.''

She propped her head on his shoulder. ''Where are they now?''

''Her highness went back to your daughter's bedroom. Jones is still guarding his dish for all he's worth.''

Tess lifted her chin and looked up at her lover, thinking that she had to feel a stab of pure sympathy for every woman who didn't have a man like this in her bed, one who considered his partner's pleasure as important as his own. One, despite however temporary affairs were usually conducted, she couldn't help wanting to know better...if only he would let her.

''You seem to be handy in the referee area,'' she ventured in that effort, keeping her tone light. ''Have you had to break up many fights over the years?''

The large hand that had started winding its way through her tousled hair stilled. ''A few,'' Jordan said evenly.

And that was all he said.

Her more sensible parts advised her not to push it. It was his choice, after all, they reminded her. But one small, stubborn portion of her just didn't want to listen. Not tonight. ''Tell me a little about your former job,'' she suggested, and backed up that invitation with an encouraging smile.

For a long moment, all her efforts won her was a frown. ''The whole thing's over and done with,'' he said at last. ''I don't see any reason to bring it up now.''

Her smile faded as another question surfaced, one she couldn't hold back. ''Is it just with me, Jordan, or don't you talk about the past—ever?''

He released a heavy breath. ''As far as I'm concerned, trips down memory lane are by and large a waste of time—always.''

Was that what she, herself, would be to him someday? Tess wondered. A memory better left to fade away? Maybe, she had to concede. For her part, though, she knew she would never completely forget their time together, would probably share a secret grin with herself over it long into the future.

The summer she took a lover.

She could accept that she might never cross his mind years from now, but something else about his attitude bothered her too much to let the subject drop. ''I don't think the past should ever be totally disregarded, even if it could be. It's where we all came from, what formed us, and if we leave every bit of it behind, we could risk losing a piece of ourselves.''

Jordan gazed down at her, his expression set. ''I'll take my chances,'' he replied.

''All right,'' she finally agreed, recognizing the futility of trying to change his mind. She summoned another smile. ''How about a midnight snack, since we both seem to be wide-awake?''

His mood clearly improving, Jordan flashed her a

grin. ''How about if you put that red garter belt on and...'' His voice trailed off suggestively.

''I've already worn it for you,'' she reminded him. ''Plus the dress and everything else I had on the night we were so surprisingly interrupted.'' And he had peeled everything off her, she remembered—layer by layer. The last layer mostly with his teeth.

His grin only grew. ''This time, I'd like you to wear just that scrap of lace. And nylons. And a pair of very high heels, if you wouldn't mind.''

She had to laugh. ''Is this by any chance another of your fantasies?''

''Mmm-hmm. One I happen to share with most every other red-blooded male on the face of the planet,'' he informed her in a suddenly husky drawl. ''So do it, please. And drive me crazy.''

She did. And drove him right up the wall.

JORDAN WOKE FROM a deep sleep, rolled onto his back and stretched his arms out wide. He expected a small yet hugely satisfied smile to curve his lips, one that now seemed to come as a matter of course on waking after spending a night in Tess's bed. Instead, he found his brow knitting in a frown as the vague feeling surfaced that something wasn't quite right in his world.

Not the weather, he decided when he slanted his eyes open to meet the bright light of a morning well underway. The day promised to be another excellent example of Mother Nature outfitted in her summer best. And it wasn't the fact that he was alone, either. He'd never expected to find Tess lying beside him. Judging by the angle of the sun slipping through the sheer bedroom curtains, she would have long since left for work.

No, it wasn't anything he could put a handle on, but something…

Still puzzled, he flipped back the sheet and slid his legs over the side of the bed, then sat there in his bare skin and narrowed his gaze thoughtfully as another possibility occurred to him. Could the niggling feeling of uneasiness have anything to do with the fight he'd put an end to last night? Could the two parties involved, in fact, be gearing themselves up right now for a second and even more rowdy round? Given prior events, he thought, that just might be the case.

Jordan resisted the urge to blow out an exasperated breath as he reached for the pair of dark briefs topping the rest of his clothes piled on a nearby chair and pulled them on. If he was right, he had to hope he'd be in time to save his eardrums from another bashing. Quickly crossing the room, he ran a hand through his hair to brush several strands back from his forehead, then opened the door and headed downstairs, intent on making for the kitchen, the site of the last confrontation.

But he only got as far as the bottom of the stairs when he came to an abrupt halt after a glance through the arched doorway to the living room. Moving slowly now, he quietly approached a scene that had him frankly staring. As improbable as it seemed, two animals were stretched out inches from each other in companionable silence under the sun streaming in through the tall front windows. No snarling. No glowering. Even determined indifference was nowhere in sight.

Just blessed peace.

The dog sensed his presence first and wasted no time in trotting over to offer an eager greeting. Jordan hunkered down and scratched behind one long ear. "Well, it looks as though you got around a certain female, pal."

Jones, dark eyes gleaming, enthusiastically panted out an agreeable response.

"Charmed her by growling over a food dish, did you?" Jordan shook his head. "Guess I've got no reason to doubt it." And there'd obviously been no reason to be concerned about what was happening between these two, he said to himself, recalling what had sent him hurrying to investigate. No real reason, most likely, to be concerned about anything.

Nevertheless, the nagging hint of unease lingered in the back of his mind as he showered, dressed and helped himself to a piece of leftover cherry pie for breakfast before heading back to his place with Jones tagging along. There, doing his best to disregard the stubborn feeling when he couldn't wipe it out entirely, he threw a load of laundry in the wash and mulled over what dinner fixings he would tackle on the grill that evening for Tess and himself, confident that with recent practice he'd gotten fairly handy at cooking over an open flame. His decision made, he scribbled a hasty shopping list on a notepad, then went out to water his tomato plant.

Which was precisely when he discovered that something wasn't only not quite right—but very wrong.

He'd seen the signs, he had to admit, his expression sobering as he crouched down at the bottom of the back steps. Undeniable indications even to his untrained eye that the plant was far from on the road to recovery. Hoping for the best, he had tried to ignore them. But now he couldn't, not any longer. Not when a short stack of leaves had dropped to the ground overnight, and thin branches were drooping nearly low enough to meet them in several places. The struggle to survive was clearly not going well.

Jordan wondered what he might have mistakenly done, or failed to do, even as reason told him he'd followed the recommended watering and fertilizing schedule to the hilt. What could he possibly have done differently? And, more importantly, what could he do now? Finding out if there was a more potent grade of fertilizer available was all that came to mind, and he decided it was at least worth investigating.

He watered the plant, taking care not to dislodge any more leaves, then went back into the house with a firm plan to stop by the landscaping service where Tess worked that afternoon. Maybe the man he'd met weeks earlier, who even Tess looked up to when it came to gardening know-how, could search his brain and come up with something. Anything. Maybe, Jordan thought, things weren't getting as desperate as they seemed at the moment.

Maybe.

"YOUR HANDSOME NEIGHBOR stopped in a few hours ago."

Violet Ziegler, who stood totaling the day's receipts at the cash register, wasted no time in passing that information along to Tess on her return from an afternoon of weeding flower beds and doing other small maintenance jobs around the city.

Tess couldn't help but note the curiosity glinting in the older woman's eyes, had no doubt that her private relationship with the man in question had prompted it. ''Sorry I missed him,'' she said mildly, a little surprised in spite of her deliberately casual manner that Jordan had come by. She was due at his place for dinner and hadn't expected to see him before then.

''I'm sure he was sorry, too,'' Violet replied, ''although I believe he was actually looking to speak with Hank.''

That news brought Tess up short. She cocked her head. ''Jordan came to see Hank?''

Violet nodded. ''About that little plant he took home with him a few weeks ago, I'm afraid. He said it looked worse today, a lot worse.'' Her regretfully resigned sigh spoke volumes. ''The last thing Hank wanted to do was tell him there was nothing more to be done, but he had no choice. We hated to see that young man leave looking so gloomy.''

Tess held back a sigh of her own, reminding herself that she'd anticipated this happening—both the plant's eventual demise and the fact that Jordan would take it hard. Like Hank, though, she had no miracle cure to offer.

''Maybe you could pop over when you get home and cheer him up,'' Violet suggested.

''Yes,'' Tess agreed, ''I will, um, pop over.'' But as for cheering him up, that remained to be seen, she thought. Still, she would give it a good try.

Tess remained determined to do her best in that effort after she hastily traded her work clothes for one of the brightest items in her closet—a cotton sundress gaily strewn with small daisies—and headed to Jordan's house. She'd already seen him preparing to fire up the grill from her bedroom window, so rather than making for the steps to the front door, she opened the slatted-wood gate at the side of the house and started down the narrow walkway. Nearly at her destination, she heard Jordan's deep voice coming from the rear. At first, she assumed he was chatting over the backyard fence with either one or maybe both halves of the friendly couple living on the other side of him. But the moment she got close enough to make out words and he suddenly came into view, she discovered her mistake.

What she saw then had her stopping in her tracks. What she heard had her stilling completely and just listening.

"So I can't think of anything else to do but just tell it straight, buddy," Jordan said. Dressed in faded denim, he was crouched down on his haunches in front of the plant that had taken him on a fruitless quest for help. "The experts have racked their brains and say there's nothing more to be done. *Nada.* Zip. Let's face it, they've given up on you." Reaching out, he briefly trailed a thumb under a sadly drooping branch. "But I haven't," he added, quietly yet firmly. "I'm out to prove them wrong, and by God I hope you are, too." He slapped a light hand on a knee to underscore that statement.

"I still intend to see some tomatoes growing in this backyard," Jordan continued in the next moment, "and you've got what it takes to do the job, trust me. Good soil. Fresh water. The sun shining down most every day. You've got everything going for you, everything you need to see this through." He paused, released a heavy breath. "So don't give up. Don't check out before your time."

Again he reached out a hand. "Don't settle for a

decent burial, buddy,'' he said, softly now. ''Don't do it...please.''

And at the sound of that last word, issued as one long finger carefully stroked its way over a little leaf, Tess's heart pitched forward and did a free fall. Just like that, it dropped beyond the grasp of her once determined hold on it. Suddenly it was no longer hers. Not entirely.

Not now.

Stunned by the sheer swiftness of the whole thing, she couldn't move a muscle. Even speech was impossible. At that moment, all she could do was stand as still as a statue while her mind raced with thoughts of the totally unexpected wisdom she had just acquired in the blink of an eye.

For weeks, she'd been walking an invisible tightrope, she now recognized. It was the narrow line separating the physical from the emotional, the thin, taut thread of basic humanness dividing pure pleasure of the senses and far deeper feelings. Caught up in the pleasure, relishing the taking, and the giving, of it, she hadn't even been aware of how shaky her position was until she'd come crashing down.

For some people, the high-wire act might be easily accomplished and effortlessly maintained. But not for her. At least not when it came to a far-from-ordinary man.

Jordan Trask.

Tess sighed a breathless sigh, accepting the undeniable truth that she had done something she'd never thought of doing, not from the very first moment she'd mulled over the possibility of starting an affair. No, she hadn't considered it, expected it, wanted it. But it had happened, anyway.

Headlong and heart first, she'd tumbled straight into love with her lover. Her temporary lover.

And she knew full well it was the forever kind of love.

Chapter Ten

Saturdays were the best days. At least that was Jordan's current opinion. Lately, that particular day of the week had been especially good to him, he couldn't help thinking as he loaded a small cooler with ice-cold cans of beer and soda plucked from his refrigerator.

He'd first come to Harmony on a Saturday, he remembered. Aunt Abigail's Bed-and-Breakfast had greeted him with friendly good cheer, and a cozy room complete with a plump feather bed had provided his first decent night's sleep in months. He'd been, he could see in hindsight, a man living on his nerves, someone who hadn't taken any real time out in years to just relax and enjoy what came his way. Burned-out, his superiors had contended, looking grim and nodding wisely. And, of course, they'd been right.

Now he'd learned to kick back and simply enjoy life, finally, although the relaxing part of the package would get to him sooner or later, he knew. Not that he wasn't getting plenty of exercise. He worked out most mornings and ran on a regular basis to stay in shape. Physically, he was as fit as ever.

But he had to do more with his life in order to find

real satisfaction in it. Kicking back for too long would have him champing at the bit for some firmly directed action. He was well aware of that. He needed a purpose, a challenge.

He needed a job worth doing.

Trouble was, he still hadn't hit on which direction to take, what sort of work to tackle next in a bid to meet those needs. But he would, he assured himself, and his back was hardly against the wall. A good part of summer remained to map out a plan. Money was no problem, either, not with the healthy savings account he'd had transferred to Harmony's largest bank.

And he *was* enjoying the present.

Jordan grinned a wholly male and distinctly gratified grin as vivid memories of other recent Saturdays flashed through his mind. The morning he'd first met his next-door neighbor...the evening he'd first kissed her...the night he'd first made love to her...

Oh, yeah. Saturday had become his downright favorite day of the week, no contest, and this one promised to be another winner. He'd already started it off right, with Tess writhing under him. Jeez, he loved to make her moan.

His grin only grew when the kitchen phone rang. He had an excellent hunch as to who was calling before he grabbed up the receiver and heard a soft voice berating him from the word "hi."

"Are you going to get the lead out? I've got a picnic lunch packed, and the lot at the park will be jammed if we don't get there soon."

Jordan leaned against the counter. "Sure you don't want to go back to bed and spend the day, um, relaxing?"

"Oh, no, you don't. We *relaxed* too long this

morning. That's why we're behind schedule. We're going to the Heritage Days festival," he was told in no uncertain terms. "And we have to go now."

He heaved an exaggerated sigh. "All right, neighbor. I've got the cooler filled. We can leave in five minutes."

"Okay. Why don't you bring Jones over?" she suggested. "He can spend the day here with Roxy."

"I'll do that," Jordan said, his grin returning in full force as he hung up a second later, because he had no doubts at all about the fact that he and his pet would also be spending the night. Moving quickly now, he dumped a layer of ice cubes over the cooler's contents and shut it with a solid thud, then crossed to the back door, opened it in a flash and stuck his head out.

"Time to come in, pal," he called to the dog standing at the far rear of the yard, where the fence met a narrow alley before well-tended backyards belonging to homes on the next street began on the other side. "We've got to get the lead out," he said, with a mental bow to the way Tess had phrased it.

Unfortunately, the dog didn't respond as expected, didn't even turn his head at the sound of his master's voice. He just stood there, facing the fence, short legs braced and furry chin lifted in a tense pose, as though he'd either heard or sensed something lurking on the other side, something that had put him on edge. Far from its usual happy wagging, his tail was as strangely still as the rest of him.

Puzzled, Jordan left the house and started down the steps. On the way, he took time to drop a glance down at the plant he'd treated to a pep talk as a last resort. No newly fallen leaves were scattered on the ground, he noted, choosing to take that as a hopeful sign. Thin branches still sagged sharply under the burden of what leaves remained, although maybe not quite so badly. He could be kidding himself on that score, he acknowledged, but maybe he'd at least accomplished a little good.

And maybe Tess didn't actually think he'd totally lost it—a conclusion he'd come to on discovering her silently watching him conduct a one-way conversation. Thrown for a loop, that was how she'd looked staring down at him, he had to admit, although she'd recovered quickly enough once he'd launched a two-way discussion on the finer points of grilling fresh trout for dinner.

If she didn't think he'd lost it, though, why had he caught her studying him more than once since that occasion, and always with an odd expression he couldn't even begin to figure out? Then again, Jordan reminded himself, she hadn't said a word about the whole thing, so why waste time speculating? No man had ever completely figured women out—and none ever would. He was dead sure of that.

Right now, one particular member of the female half of the population was probably tapping a slender foot and studying the clock. He wasn't earning any points by keeping her waiting. Too bad Jones clearly had his own priorities.

"What's the matter, pal?" Jordan asked as he crossed the grassy yard with quick strides.

Jones growled softly in reply, his attention still locked on the fence and what might lurk beyond it.

Jordan glanced past the dog and saw nothing out of the ordinary. Nevertheless, he'd been taught to accept little at first glance, and old habits had him moving closer and aiming a thoroughly appraising gaze up and down the alley. Still nothing, he thought, not so much as a stray paper wrapper fluttering in the breeze or scraping a path over the smooth asphalt lined with well-maintained trash cans. As peaceful—not to mention tidy—scenes went, this was a perfect example.

Jordan took a step back and looked down at his companion. "If there was something there, it's gone, believe me."

Jones only growled again, obviously not convinced.

"Time to go," his master said firmly at that point, deciding enough was enough. "You get to laze around for the rest of the day with your slanty-eyed girlfriend, you lucky sonofagun."

Snorting out what seemed to be the equivalent of a canine sigh, the dog gave up then and finally turned away, but only to glance back several times as they returned to the house.

"You don't have to worry, pal," Jordan advised as they started up the steps. "Everything's fine. After all, why wouldn't it be? This is Harmony."

Despite the reassurance, Jones turned his head and looked back one last time.

HERITAGE DAYS, an annual event generally anticipated with much enthusiasm, had marked the beginning of August for generations. Traditionally held on the first weekend of that long and lazy month, it was a tribute to Harmony's past and a salute to its future. As festivals went, it was far from the largest Arizona had to offer. Still, it had several elements in common with many outdoor celebrations held throughout the fifty states, not the least of which was a host of smiles blooming on the faces of people young and old who were thoroughly engaged in the act of having a good time. Today, in a lively mix that sought to provide something for everyone, carnival rides vied with arts and crafts displays for tourist dollars, while church bake sales drew longtime residents eager to sample each other's efforts, and games geared for children too little to participate in most other activities provided a winner, and a small prize, every time.

From her seat on a wide blanket, one of several spread out in front of a large, latticed-wood gazebo painted snowy white, Tess took in the sights around her. This time last year, she'd been in almost the exact spot, she remembered. With Ali away in California, she had shared the quiet aftermath of a free-for-all picnic lunch with Sally and Ben Mendoza while their boys stretched out on the grass nearby, trading tales of the day's earlier adventures with a group of young friends.

This year, things were much the same. Except, for her, everything had changed. Because this year, the kind of man she'd never imagined would enter her life was close enough to brush elbows. Dressed in a black polo paired with khaki pants, he sat with his long legs bent at the knee and his strong arms wrapped around them. Arms that had, by now, been firmly wrapped around her too many times to count. A small part of her remained a bit amazed by that, while the rest of her was still dealing with the undeniable truth that she loved him.

Would always love him.

While the short break in lunchtime conversation continued, Tess watched as Floyd Crenshaw, his barbershop closed for the occasion, climbed the short steps to the floor of the gazebo in the company of two of his cronies. Brady Crenshaw, quickly following in his wheelchair, used well-muscled arms to propel himself up a ramp built at one side and came to a smooth stop directly in front of his father. Offering the next round in musical entertainment that had already featured the high school band, the quartet launched into "Heart Of My Heart."

It was so in tune with what was foremost in her mind, Tess had to wonder at the timing, had to admit that she'd again deliberately worn her daisy-print sundress, its full skirt topped by a fitted bodice sporting narrow shoulder straps, to provide some cheer—not for Jordan's benefit this time, but for her own. Finding one's heart had given itself to a man who would take a piece of it with him when he left was hardly a woman's fondest wish come true, she couldn't deny. Nevertheless, it had happened and now she had to deal with it. So she would.

Not that he was leaving yet. She still had what remained of the summer before she had to let him go. It would be enough, because it had to be enough. And she wouldn't waste a minute of it being sorry, she'd already decided. Regrets at this point would only spoil their remaining time together. She didn't intend to do anything so foolish. No matter what, she would enjoy being with him while she could.

Then the life she'd carefully planned for herself and her daughter would go on. She would be the proud owner of her own business before much longer. She would make a success of it, too. And she would continue to be the best mother she knew how to be. Whatever the future had in store, Ali would have everything she needed to blossom from a healthy, happy child into a budding young woman.

Everything except a father, an inner voice reminded her. But fate, she knew, had taken that out of her hands.

As an enthusiastic round of applause signaled the song's end, Tess joined in and glanced up at a suddenly shaded sun, noting that a line of fluffy white clouds had drifted in from the low mountains to the east. Rain was a distinct possibility, she concluded, recognizing the signs, but not until much later.

"Good music," Sally said when another tune started, this one performed to a livelier beat as a guitar was added to the mix. "Too bad there's no place to dance."

Jordan blew out a rueful breath. "Thank God there's no place to dance," he countered.

Sally laughed. "You did all right, as I recall."

"Not hardly," he replied. "The big Texan you married is the smooth operator in that department."

Grinning, Ben accepted the compliment with a casual shrug of hefty shoulders outlined by a striped golf shirt. "Since I can't strut my stuff," he drawled, "I suppose I'll have to make do with a second beer."

"Good thinking. Have one of mine this time." Jordan pulled two cans from the cooler resting on the grass beside him and lightly tossed one over. "Anything for you, ladies?"

Both shook their heads.

"I'm stuffed," Sally added, patting a stomach left bare by her navy halter top.

"You ate too much of your special fried chicken," her husband teased before silence again settled on the group. With the buzz of quiet conversations going on around them, they listened to the music drifting on a warm breeze that gently swayed the branches of scattered trees.

Jordan tipped his head back and took a short swallow from his can, thinking that the day had turned out to be a winner, just as he'd anticipated. He'd talked Tess into joining him for an earlier ride on the towering Ferris wheel, shouting with laughter while she'd shrieked in his ear when he'd rocked the seat at the very top of it, after which his knack for leveling a line of plastic milk bottles with a battered baseball had netted him a large stuffed animal as his prize. It was a plump pig, a bright purple porker, that squealed like a blaring siren when squeezed, and it was as ugly as sin, at least in his opinion. But Tess had actually seemed thrilled with it when he'd presented it to her with a mock formal bow.

No, he told himself as another song came to a close, he'd never figure out the female half of the planet. Still, that didn't mean he wasn't hoping to be further rewarded for his efforts after they got home and he got Tess to himself. With any luck at all, he'd—

"Now, don't you young lads drink too much beer," a soft voice coming from above him cautioned, breaking into Jordan's thoughts. "A small dose of spirits is fine to mark a celebration, but a big one will make your handsome heads hurt."

Glancing up, it didn't take him long to recognize the new arrival as the elderly silver-haired woman probably close to eighty who had once picked out a cantaloupe for him. Today she wore a deep blue shirtwaist dress that all but matched wide eyes thinly framed by gold-rimmed glasses and twinkling with wry good humor.

"Hello, Miss Hester," Sally greeted warmly and went on to officially introduce Jordan to Hester Goodbody, who'd taught for many years at Harmony's oldest and largest elementary school.

"Pleased to meet you, ma'am," he said, getting to his feet and offering a smile. Easily twice the size of the small-boned woman standing before him, he still hadn't quite gotten over the novelty of being referred to as a *young lad.*

"Ah, what a bonny smile you have," she told him as a surprisingly firm handshake was completed. "I always say a happy face shows one's best side to the world."

"I remember that from first grade," Tess said, viewing them both with a lifted chin and obvious amusement. "Won't you join us? There's room and plenty of food left over."

The veteran teacher shook her head. "Thank you, dear, but there's so much to do. I'm supervising the games for the wee ones, you know. I only stopped by to... Well," she continued after a brief hesitation, "a thought came to me as I was crossing the lawn, one involving our newcomer." Her gaze slid back to Jordan for an instant, then returned to Tess. Bending now, she murmured something in her former pupil's ear.

When two sets of baby blues proceeded to lock on him, Jordan felt the rapid urge to turn and run while he could, as he had on a memorable occasion with Tess's daughter. Unfortunately for his peace of mind, that urge grew as a gradual smile curved Tess's lips. Only that morning, he'd been tasting those lips to his content. Right now, the sight had him bracing for disaster.

"Miss Hester," Tess said after a long moment, still staring up at him, "I believe that's a truly brilliant idea."

But Jordan didn't think so. Not at all.

Not when they sprang it on him without further ado. Not when Sally and Ben promptly bought into the plan. Not even after he'd finally caved in and found himself making his way across the park with Tess walking beside him. "Why did I let you talk me into this?" he muttered.

"Because it's in a good cause."

"Humph" was all Jordan could come up with in reply.

Which was the extent of conversation before they reached a tentlike booth with an open front that was lined up with several others displaying a variety of arts and crafts. This one was definitely different, though—not in appearance, but in what it offered to everyone willing to part with a dollar, with all proceeds donated to charity.

This booth sold kisses.

Currently manning it was the couple who lived on the other side of the home Jordan had rented. He'd already chatted with Donna and David Richards on more than one occasion, sharing casual conversation over the back fence when they happened to wind up outside at the same time. The lanky, fair-haired man and his petite brunette wife didn't look old enough to be parents of a son nearing college age, but that was undeniably the case.

"Are we by any chance being relieved?" David

asked the new arrivals as they approached, plainly looking enthused at the prospect.

''Yeah,'' Jordan said shortly, noting that no customers were around right this minute. Maybe none would show up for whatever time he had to spend here. He could only hope. He was as ready to do a good deed for a worthwhile charity as the next person, but he wasn't all that comfortable doing this one. Hell, if it would keep customers away, he'd gladly reach deep into his own pockets for a hefty donation to make up for the lack of business. Unfortunately, he was a long way from sure that would work.

He also wasn't too sure how he felt about other men kissing Tess practically under his nose, even for the best of causes. If one of them lingered too long over it, he supposed he'd find out.

Viewing him with her head cocked at a wry angle, Donna chuckled softly. ''Don't look so glum,'' she told him. ''We've actually been having a good time.''

The men shared a look, one that spoke volumes.

''Can't wait to do it again next year,'' David threw in, rolling his eyes.

What the guy probably couldn't wait for was a cold beer in his immediate future, Jordan thought sourly, deciding then and there to have another one himself after this deal was over. Resigned to his fate for the moment, he walked around the small booth topped with hanging loops of colorful plastic streamers. He entered through a long flap in the heavy fabric at the back, then held it open for Tess to slide through behind him. Twin padded folding chairs occupied opposite ends, while two large glass jars stood on a narrow counter at the front, each nearly half filled with treasury bills.

"Looks like it's been a profitable day so far," Tess said, studying them.

"It has," Donna agreed, "although things fell off once lunchtime came around."

"Well, we have to go," David said, obviously more than ready to hustle himself and his wife out of there.

"First, I have to do my share," Donna said, and took a dollar bill from a jeans pocket to toss it into the jar marked *His* in several places with bold scarlet letters. "I'll be your first customer," she told Jordan. Standing on tiptoes, she pursed rose-shaded lips and waited for him to plant one on her, which he did, lightly and briefly.

"You know," she added in a low murmur, poised to turn toward where her husband held the cloth flap open, "I have to confess that I saw something I never expected to see when I got up early one morning weeks ago to get a head start on putting in my new herb garden." Her eyes sparkled at the memory. "Usually birds are the only ones up at that hour. So you can imagine my surprise when someone suddenly appeared and hopped over a nearby fence to pick a flower." She paused for a meaningful beat. "It was, ah, quite a sight."

Then she was gone, slipping out through the flap, and Jordan was left to stare at the rear of the booth and recall exactly what he'd been wearing—or hadn't been wearing—when he'd stormed over that fence for a yellow rose at the crack of dawn in his underwear. Jeez.

Tess, who'd clearly heard the whole thing, sputtered out a muffled laugh. "I'll bet that *was* a sight."

He shot her a sidelong look and kept his back to

the front of the booth, telling himself that he wasn't blushing. At least he damn well hoped he wasn't.

"How long before we get rescued, er, relieved?" he asked, keeping his tone mild.

Something drew his companion's attention just then and had her angling a glance past his shoulder. "I think," she replied after a second, still looking beyond him, "that we're going to be here for a while. Or, at least you are."

He was?

Jordan inched his way around and found his wary gaze taking in the sight of Hester Goodbody, who calmly stood at the counter directly in front of the *His* jar, a dollar bill held in one delicately boned hand. Plainly she was his next customer.

But not his only customer. Not hardly. As short and slender as she was, he had no trouble seeing behind her, and what he saw was a line of women of every age, size and description that stretched back a long, long way.

"Definitely a brilliant idea, Miss Hester," Tess said wryly from beside him. "Looks like we'll have plenty to donate to charity this year."

SHE TEASED HIM about it all the way home, feeling more carefree than she had in days. Every now and then, she gave the stuffed animal taking up most of her lap a light squeeze out of sheer devilment, and cheerfully grinned at the sound of each little squeal.

She'd already decided to name her brand-new pet Precious. Precious, the fuzzy purple pig. Wondering how Roxy would take the new addition and whether the cat would try to make mincemeat of it, she ventured another squeeze.

''Do that one more time and I'm tossing it out the window,'' Jordan grumbled as he turned onto a narrow street that would wind its way around to their final destination.

''I don't think it would fit through the window.'' Tess angled her gaze his way, noted that he looked slightly frayed around the edges. *Enough teasing,* wisdom said. But she just couldn't stop. Not yet.

''You'll feel better after I feed you dinner,'' she told him mildly. ''Kissing all those women probably worked up an appetite.''

''Humph,'' was his short reply.

She tucked her tongue in her cheek. ''Maybe you need some lip balm, too.''

That produced a sidelong look stern enough to have her backing off, at last. ''Okay, no more joking.''

''About time,'' Jordan muttered as he turned into his driveway and cut the engine.

Tess hopped out, still holding the plump pig. A glance up at the sky found only the same fluffy scattered clouds she'd seen at lunchtime, tinged pink now. It was still a beautiful day, even as sunset approached. ''I thought we were in for a storm, but I guess not,'' she told Jordan as he hoisted the white foam cooler from his trunk.

''Let's go to my place first,'' he said, stepping back to let her close the trunk. ''I'll dump this out, and you can restock the refrigerator with the leftover cans while I put the Explorer in the garage for the night.''

''All right,'' Tess agreed.

''And then,'' he added, finally looking more cheerful, ''I plan on being rewarded for what I went through today.''

She lifted a brow. ''With dinner?''

His lips took a wicked curve. ''For starters.''

They were both grinning in anticipation of events to come when they mounted the steps to the front porch. Jordan set the cooler down only long enough to retrieve his key and open the door, then hoisted it again and shouldered his way in, with Tess quickly following behind. She nudged the door shut and started down the narrow hallway, headed for the rear of the house in Jordan's wake.

Unfortunately, neither of them made it as far as the kitchen. Fate had something else in store as a man suddenly appeared in the arched doorway to the living room and brought both of them to a rapid halt.

The sight sent Tess's pulse racing in a flash. Startled into total stillness, she could only stand there and stare at someone who was a complete stranger to her. Black haired, dark eyed, taller than average, and wearing a well-tailored ivory linen suit over a silky tan T-shirt, he might be viewed by many as attractive, in a suave, swarthy way.

But then, Tess thought, many wouldn't currently be facing the weapon he held in long-fingered hands covered by thin latex gloves. It looked different from any gun she'd ever seen—most of them in the movies, where good and bad guys fought it out to the finish. Still she recognized the danger it posed, felt the air around her all but crackling with it.

She had no doubt that this was one of the bad guys.

''Hello, Trask,'' he said in the next breath, his lips twisting in a slow, sly smile that gradually displayed a string of gleaming white teeth. ''I told you we'd meet again someday, but I bet you didn't believe me.''

Chapter Eleven

No, he hadn't believed. But he'd been wrong, and now a smug slice of pure slime had wound up on his doorstep.

"Hello, scumbag," Jordan bit out, keeping his hands locked around the cooler's handles. He would have liked nothing more than to put a fast fist into the smirking face, but he'd learned that brawn alone wasn't the answer when it came to dealing with a loaded weapon. It also took brains to get the job done.

The other man's sly smile only widened, like a wily shark's. "Where are your manners, Trask?" he asked, his voice low and cultured, with no discernible accent. "You haven't even introduced me to the lady."

Keep her out of this, Jordan wanted to roar, and knew he'd only be yielding another weapon to be used against him if he even hinted that Tess was anything more than an acquaintance. So he kept his silence and contented himself with a steely stare.

"Ah, well. I suppose I'll have to do it myself. Felix Raine," he continued with a brief nod in Tess's direction.

"Tess Cameron," was the soft reply he received after a short pause. Her voice didn't tremble, Jordan noted, though she must be scared out of her wits. Nothing remotely like this had ever happened to her before. He was dead sure on that score.

"Too bad we had to meet under such troubling circumstances," Felix murmured. "But then, sometimes these things can't be helped." Switching his gaze back to Jordan, he added, "It doesn't surprise me that you haven't asked how I got in here. Your locks would hardly be a challenge for a novice. I did expect to have to deal with your dog, but fortunately the animal proved to be nowhere around when I came through the back door and searched the place."

"You were in the alley this morning," Jordan said, remembering earlier events.

"Yes, and your mutt managed to get a glimpse of me while I was checking out the lay of the land, so to speak." With that, he took a careful step back, keeping his gaze steady. "Now I suggest you and Ms. Cameron join me in the living room. I'm sure you'll want to put down your burden, Trask. It must be getting heavy."

He would rather have kept it. At least it provided something to throw at the creep, assuming he got the chance to do it. But Jordan realized this was no time to argue. He'd be far better off putting his mind to the task of finding a way to get Tess out of this mess. Her safety was vital.

And his own presence in Harmony had placed it in question. There was no way he could avoid that conclusion. If he'd never come here, she would never have been put at risk.

God, he'd never forgive himself if anything happened to her. That thought hammered through him. The fault would be flatly his if she suffered because of his decision to try out a whole new kind of life. He'd put her in harm's way, however unwittingly, and nothing would change that fact, not even if they both came through this without so much as a scratch.

No, he wasn't sure he would ever forgive himself. Period.

As the other man slowly retreated, Jordan stepped forward into the living room, forcing his thoughts back to the matter at hand, and carefully laid the cooler on the carpet. Straightening, he tossed a glance behind him, and was almost startled to find Tess's arms still wrapped around that ugly pig as she quietly walked forward to stand beside him. He'd forgotten completely about it.

"I won't ask you to sit down," Felix said, his attention on Jordan. "You'll make a better target standing."

He squared his shoulders. "You should have opted for a real pistol if you wanted to shoot up the place, Raine."

"So you recognize it." Felix nodded. "Somehow, I thought you would. For the lady's benefit, though, I'll explain that it's a dart gun."

"A dart gun," Tess repeated cautiously.

"For tranquilizing wild animals, usually. But I have no doubt it will work quite nicely on the man who was so instrumental in sending me to jail."

"Where drug runners belong," Jordan said grimly.

Felix shrugged. "The courts decided otherwise. But only after I spent several months behind bars. My first time in a cage and it wasn't a pleasant experience, Trask. That's why I have it in mind for you. That, in fact, is why I plan on putting a dart in your tough hide. When you eventually wake up, we'll both be far south of here. You'll be the one in a cage by that time and some associates who owe me a few favors will see that you stay there until I decide what to do with you next—which I assure you, will take a satisfying long time.'' He breathed out a thin sigh. ''My only regret is that I'll have to make sure the lady accompanies us now. But, as I said, sometimes these things can't be helped.''

Everything inside Jordan clenched even as he intentionally assumed a casual stance and crossed his arms over his chest. ''Seems like that would be more trouble than it's worth,'' he replied with deliberate mildness. ''Why not just lock her in a closet and be done with it, since I'm the one you really want?''

Felix chuckled low in his throat. ''Nice try, Trask, but any choice in the matter ended the second she saw my face. Witnesses can be extremely inconvenient.'' He shook his head slowly. ''No, both of you are going to have to...disappear.''

Tess drew in a breath as that last word hovered in the air, and silently waited for her nerves to start screaming. Instead, they remained surprisingly quiet. Maybe, she reflected, because there was little question in her mind that, despite his outward calm, Jordan was taking recent events very seriously, waiting for something—anything—that would allow him to spring into action and get them both safely out of this fix.

No, she had little doubt about that. The only real question she found she had at the moment was, *could she help?*

Not when it came to the weapon being used against them, she didn't hesitate to admit. Despite having one dart at his immediate disposal and two people to currently contend with, Jordan's nemesis clearly had the upper hand. That had to be the case, because even if they both rushed him at the same time, he would pull the trigger and launch that dart at Jordan. And if she mustered every ounce of courage she possessed and did the rushing on her own...he would still launch it at Jordan. Nothing else made sense, because he didn't need her drugged to control her. Physically she was hardly a match for him.

So rushing him was out, a conclusion Jordan had probably long since reached. It might work in an action movie. This, however, was another story, and as long as that gun was firmly trained on Jordan, the odds were in the bad guy's favor.

But, Tess thought in the next breath, if she could manage to provide a distraction, enough of one to win a certain man's undivided attention for a few seconds, Jordan might well be able to put it to good use. It had to be worth a try.

Not that distracting Mr. Suave would be easy, she acknowledged, stroking one hand absently down the purple pig's soft belly as she mulled things over. It would probably mean taking him completely by surprise. Something in her own favor, reason said, was that she knew her nerves were steady. And she was the only one who knew it. Could she use that fact to her advantage? Could—

Tess's hand stopped in mid-stroke as another thought hit, one that had her struggling to keep her expression blank. She had a second, and perhaps even greater advantage. Good Lord, she was holding it at this moment.

The man with the gun had no way of knowing that her brand-new pet could squeal like a, well, stuck pig. It could, she was absolutely positive, produce one dandy of a surprise. And it would probably produce an even bigger one if the bad guy were already on edge, rattled in some way, when the squealing started, she allowed on further consideration. But how to accomplish that? By getting on *his* nerves? It was all she could come up with, and this just might be where her other advantage came in.

Tess reached inside herself and called on every scrap of acting ability she had. However meager, it would have to be enough, and her only comfort was that she hadn't actually failed her high-school drama class.

Venturing what she hoped was a passable sob of pure anguish, she took a small sidestep away from Jordan, then sniffed for all she was worth. Genuine tears, as hard as she tried to produce a few, proved to be beyond her. Some people could probably cry on command. She obviously wasn't one of them.

''You can't take me with you,'' she said at last, doing her best to choke out the words. ''I have to stay here. I have responsibilities. I have a *daughter.*'' Which she would never have revealed if Ali hadn't been hundreds of miles from here, yet the fact that it was true as far as it went made her sound more convincing. To her ears, at any rate.

Felix Raine aimed a narrow-eyed glance her way but didn't allow it to linger. ''Getting upset at this point won't change anything,'' he said coolly.

Upset? The clear dismissal in his tone, as if she were no more than a pesky fly to be brushed aside, just strengthened her determination to do everything she could to help foil him. He hadn't even begun to see how upset she could get, she thought. But he would.

"You don't understand," she went on desperately, letting her voice rise several notches. "My little girl will be left without a mother."

She supposed even bad guys had mothers who cared about them, but this particular one didn't so much as look at her. Not this time. And she couldn't risk looking at Jordan. She was afraid she'd give herself away, because a real actress she wasn't, and she knew it.

Still, she wasn't giving up.

"You can't be so heartless," she all but wailed now, taking another small step from the man at her side. If—no, *when,* she firmly amended—the time came, he would need room to move swiftly. And she was certain he could do exactly that.

The sheer volume of her last statement won her another, and slightly more intent, glance. "I suggest you calm down," Felix muttered, his jaw growing rigid with the words.

She was getting to him. He no longer looked so coolly in charge of his temper. Too bad she couldn't take time to enjoy her success, though, because something told her she'd better throw herself into the final act before he decided to launch that dart at Jordan so he'd be free to shut her up.

"You're telling me to calm down!" she shouted in the next breath. At the top of her lungs. "I'm about to be *kidnapped,* hauled off to heaven knows where, and you want me to...oh."

She let her voice falter to a halt, rolled her eyes and dropped her chin to her chest in a bid to do a halfway believable impression of a dead faint. Then, as her knees buckled, she pitched straight forward, facedown, letting go of Precious the Pig at the last minute. But only to land squarely on it. The result was an earsplitting squeal that threatened to rattle the windows. Yes!

She heard the rough clash of hard-muscled bodies meeting before she even had time to raise her head. Grunts and growls soon followed. The fight she watched, still lying full length on the carpet, was short. And sweet, as it turned out. Because Jordan was the clear victor after no more than several powerful and well-placed punches. When it was over, he kicked the gun that had fallen to the floor across the room and stood with his fists still clenched, staring daggers down at what was now a totally unconscious man, one who currently looked far less suave with blood dripping from a battered lip.

Hopping up, Tess rushed toward her lover and threw her arms around his neck when he did a half turn to face her. "Thank God you weren't shot." She rested her forehead on a broad shoulder, took in the comforting feel of him. "I was so worried."

"And upset," he added soberly, running a soothing hand down her back. "I know. And I'm sorry, Tess."

Upset. There was that word again. Clinging to him, it dawned on her that he actually believed at least a part of the act she'd been putting on. Not the faint. He would know that was a sham, because it would have taken Superwoman to recover that quickly. But he had expected her to be scared witless.

Then again, so had she.

Grateful, and undeniably proud, to have discovered she was made of sterner stuff when push came to shove, she pulled back and looked him straight in the eye. "I was worried—terribly—but not hysterical, or anywhere near it, thankfully." She hadn't been able to cry a drop, but now found she had no trouble smiling, widely. "Oh, Jordan, we did it." For some reason, she wanted to jump up and down, like a child on Christmas morning. "We got the bad guy!" She had to hug him, long and hard, just for the sheer joy of it.

"Yes, we got him. You did great." The words warmed her, yet his tone remained more than sober enough to tell her he wasn't nearly as jubilant as she was. That much was clear even before she pulled back again and studied his set in concrete expression. No, he wasn't happy. At all.

"Why don't you call the police?" he suggested evenly, releasing her. "I'll tie the scumbag up."

Her smile faded. "Okay," she said, and stepped back at last. "Is everything all right?" she couldn't help asking.

He only offered the barest nod in reply before stripping off his belt with smooth efficiency and bending over his captive.

She made the call, calmly explained the situation to the dispatcher who answered, and fully expected that the veteran head of Harmony's small police force would choose to involve himself from the start, which meant things would be handled thoroughly and professionally once he arrived in short order. There was no reason to worry any longer, she thought, sighing softly as she hung up. But recalling Jordan's expression, she couldn't quite believe it.

No matter what reason said, something inside her told her that everything was not *all right.*

IT WAS LATE when they left Harmony's downtown area and started for home after helping the wheels of law enforcement grind to a satisfactory conclusion and catching a quick dinner of fast-food tacos at a small corner stand near the police station. The hasty meal was a far cry from the cozy one Tess had intended to fix, but neither of them had been all that hungry, anyway. Jordan had actually eaten less than she had. She aimed a probing glance his way from her seat beside him as they drove down a dark road. He appeared to be no happier than he had hours earlier. She was almost getting used to that set in concrete expression. Unfortunately.

"We can have dessert when we get back," she said, more to fill a growing void in the conversation than anything. "There's some of the pie I made a few days ago left."

She knew he was partial to her baking. Still she wasn't surprised when he shook his head. "I'll settle for a brandy. Luckily, your father and I didn't polish off my entire supply."

She couldn't deny that he looked as though he could use a stiff drink. And deserved one, too. As evenings went, she thought, this was definitely one to remember. At least things had gone well at police headquarters, which was due in large part to Jordan's efforts.

Tom Kennedy, Harmony's longtime police chief, had personally taken their statements, which Jordan had promptly backed up with a phone call to a veteran Border Patrol official, who'd gladly offered an account of Felix Raine's past misdeeds, along with a candid comment about hoping the SOB stayed in jail this time. Tom, reclining with deceptive ease in an old swivel chair set behind a sturdy mahogany desk, had listened with shrewdly narrowed eyes and then calmly vowed to do his damnedest to make sure that happened.

Hard on the heels of that conversation, the van found parked in the alley behind Jordan's place had provided a new twist when Jordan's tip that it might contain hidden cargo proved to be true after a thorough search. Raine hadn't been careful enough to use those latex gloves to keep his fingerprints off a bag filled with a very illegal substance, which had led to narcotics charges being added to assault and attempted kidnapping.

"Looks like my current guest will be spending a good long time in a federal prison," Tom had drawled, thumbing back the wide-brimmed, Western-style hat he favored to cover his increasingly receding hairline. "One thing for sure, my department won't give the courts any excuse to overturn another conviction." He'd smiled like a fox as he bid Tess and Jordan good-night at the double doors to the brick building housing the station. "Pleasure meeting you, Trask," he'd said, then traded a silent look with Tess before gently telling her to take care.

Once, looking far more grim, Tom had rung her doorbell and delivered news that had not only rocked her world but shocked her to the core. It was a day she would never forget, she knew, just as she would never forget the events of the past few hours. This time, though, she'd been able to do something—act rather than react—and she *was* proud of how she'd handled it. She was even prouder of the man seated beside her, and could only regret that he wasn't more pleased with the way things had turned out.

She didn't know what was bothering him...but something was.

The moment Jordan slid his key in the lock a short while later, Jones issued a warning bark. ''It's me, pal,'' he said. ''He's probably been right there since we left,'' Jordan added, opening the front door.

''Standing guard,'' Tess summed up with a nod. She didn't doubt it. Earlier, after giving her initial account of events to the police chief and two uniformed officers, she'd checked on the animals, put Precious the Pig in a closet for safekeeping after the cat seemed a bit too eager to investigate the new addition, and brought the dog back from her place just in time to get a gratifying look at a still groggy Felix Raine being hauled out of Jordan's house in handcuffs. Jones had taken great exception to the prisoner on sight, straining at his leash and growling to beat the band.

''The bad guy's behind bars,'' she told the dog now. ''You can take a break.''

Jordan closed the door behind them, bent and offered a reassuring pat. ''She's right.''

Jones licked his master's hand, but didn't linger when Jordan straightened. Instead, he moved away, plopped himself down across the threshold and returned to guard duty, as if he wasn't taking any chances.

''Let him be for the moment,'' Jordan said. He raked a hand through his hair and started for the rear of the house. ''Want to have a brandy with me?''

''No, thanks,'' Tess replied, walking beside him, ''but I'll keep you company.'' What she wanted, longed for, was his arms around her—to be held by him, and to hold him, as well. Most of all, though, she longed for his expression to lighten enough to tell her that the worst of this evening was over.

She continued to wait for some sort of sign as she leaned against the counter and watched him pour a short dose of amber liquor into a small crystal glass. Unfortunately, even after a hearty swallow, his face retained its stony cast.

"Let's go out in the yard," he suggested, turning toward the back door, glass in hand. "The air in here reeks of him."

Tess didn't have to ask who *he* was, didn't mention the fact that she herself smelled nothing unusual. "All right," she agreed calmly, and followed Jordan out the door.

And then she watched again, standing on the back steps, as he steadily paced the yard. This time, she couldn't make out much more than his restlessly roaming body. They hadn't switched on an outside light, and thickening clouds overhead hid any trace of moon and stars. The warm wind, which had picked up throughout the evening, fluttered her full skirt around her knees. It hadn't stormed yet. But it would, she thought. And probably blow through and be gone long before morning. She could only hope that whatever was troubling the man she did her best to view in the nearly total darkness would pass as quickly.

All at once Jordan changed course in midstep, headed her way and came to a halt directly in front of her. With her perched on the first step, they were eye to eye, and for a hushed moment they just stared at each other. Then he sighed, long and hard. "You'd be better off to go home, Tess," he told her quietly yet bluntly. "I won't be decent company anytime soon."

She drew in a breath, let it out. "What's wrong,

Jordan?'' It was the question she'd wanted to ask for hours, one she couldn't hold back any longer.

His gaze didn't waver. ''Everything.''

Everything. She had to blink, startled by the sheer scope of that single ground-out word. Everything? What in the world did he mean by—

''Go home,'' he repeated, breaking into her thoughts, making it a near order this time. ''Just turn around, go back to your place, and let me handle this on my own.'' He paused for a beat. ''Because if you stay, I'm going to...''

Desire, swift and stark, edged those last words, roughening his voice. She welcomed the sound, well aware of what he hadn't gone on to say. For the first time in hours, he was showing genuine emotion, and of a particular kind that had her pulse leaping in response.

This she could deal with, she told herself, pushing every other thought from her mind. This she could answer with her own growing longing to be as close to him as she could get. Without hesitation, she took the small glass he held in one large hand, bent and carefully set it at one side of the steps. Then she straightened, reached out with both hands and slowly slid her palms up the muscled wall of his chest, again gazing straight into his eyes.

''I'm staying.''

She expected his arms to close around her in a solid grasp, expected his firm mouth to come down on hers, expected him to kiss her, deeply and hungrily. Not only expected it, but rejoiced in every sensation.

But she didn't expect what followed, never suspected they would wind up stretched out on the cool, crisp grass in a matter of moments. And never so much as imagined he would start undressing her, then and there.

They were apparently—no, definitely, she amended—going to make love outside, in the open, on the ground, in the middle of a quiet family neighborhood. Right this minute.

Tess considered being shocked, found herself tugging at his clothes instead while she arched closer and returned his kiss with everything she had. Fireworks. She wanted more of them, more of him. And she wanted to give in return, badly. So when he lifted his head at last and let them both take in a breath, she gasped out one short statement, and truly meant it, because she wasn't stopping.

"Heavens, I hope the neighbors are asleep!"

Jordan merely groaned a reply. The power of speech had already deserted him. Awareness of his surroundings was rapidly fading, as well. At the moment, he could scarcely think. Not that his rapidly flagging thought processes were necessary when it came to understanding something right down to his bones.

He needed Tess, and he needed her *now*.

Intent on meeting that need with all the speed at his command, he nevertheless managed somehow to get her out of her dress without tearing the thin fabric to shreds, and even retained enough common sense to retrieve protection from his wallet before his clothing went the way of hers to land in scattered piles on the grass. Somehow, too, he succeeded in resisting the potent urge to surrender to sheer male greed and gentled his touch as much as he could as he forged an intimate path over silky bare skin, again and again, first with his hands, then with his mouth.

But once he accepted an unmistakable invitation issued to the tune of gratifyingly familiar little moans and slipped inside with one long thrust, any semblance of control was totally beyond him. He not only needed, he had to have.

Now his blood roared in his ears. *Deeper, faster, more.* The words repeated in his brain as his body's demands swamped him. For the first time in all the times they'd been together, he didn't know whether Tess was fully with him in the quest for satisfaction, didn't—couldn't—care.

Then she shuddered under him, clinging to him in a tight tangle of arms and legs, and he swallowed her soft cry of release even as he surged toward his own. When it hit, every muscle in his body jerked in response, then trembled with the aftershocks before he collapsed on top of her.

Peace.

He found it…but not for long.

Reality surfaced all too soon and had Jordan levering himself away from the woman who held him in a light, warm grasp. Turning, he landed flat on his back in one quick motion, his pulse still pounding through him as he stared up at the heavy black sky. It matched, to a tee, the dark mood that rapidly reclaimed him.

He knew what he had to do, had known for hours, he admitted. The past he'd been firmly determined to leave behind had come back to haunt him. There was no getting around that fact, and no way he could guarantee history wouldn't repeat itself. The only thing he could do was make damn sure that if it did, nothing he cared about would suffer for it.

He cared about Tess Cameron.

And her tomboy-angel daughter.

And the city they both called home, one that was filled with people who had made him feel a welcome part of a friendly community for the first time in his life.

So, after debating for weeks on what road to take next, his future—at least the immediate part of that future—had just been mapped out for him. The irony of it almost made him smile. Almost.

"I guess it's time to get dressed," he murmured, and made himself get to his feet. He tugged on his clothes, heard Tess dressing beside him after a second, yet deliberately kept his gaze off her and concentrated on his shoes. The silence between them built as he started for the house, determined not to say what he had to say under the cover of darkness. He made his way to the porch, switched on the small outside light, and spoke at last when he turned and found Tess standing a few feet behind him at the top of the steps. Even fully dressed, she looked as though she'd just been ravished, lavishly.

"I'm sorry," he said. And he was, more than enough to feel the hard weight of it in his gut. "I never should have let that happen."

She didn't ask what he meant. She merely smoothed a palm over her thoroughly tousled hair and said, "I'm not sorry. Believe me. And there's no reason you should be."

Just spit it out, Trask.

"There is," he told her, "because I'm leaving Harmony. It shouldn't take me more than forty-eight hours to pack everything up and be gone."

Chapter Twelve

He was leaving. Not at the end of summer, but in a matter of hours. *Hours.*

Tess stilled completely while her mind struggled to take it in. It wasn't easy. Her senses were all but singing from the swift, sweet, glorious way he'd taken her on a wild rocket-ride to the peak of pleasure—and he was going.

Just like that. Still at a loss for words, she managed to get one out. The most important one.

"Why?"

"Because I don't belong here."

Again she was abruptly brought up short, both by the blunt statement itself and the unmistakable regret underscoring it. The latter told her that he didn't want to leave—not now, not yet—but he was going, regardless. Why, she had to ask again, making it a silent question this time as she laced her fingers tightly behind her back. What would make him pack up and leave when he wasn't ready?

And then the truth of it suddenly dawned on her. He'd said he didn't belong here, she thought, but what he'd really meant was that he didn't deserve to be here, and it all came back to what had happened today. Yes, that had to be it.

She took a deep, steadying breath. "Jordan, you weren't responsible for the bad guy—"

"The hell I wasn't," he shot back, cutting her off. "He came here because of *me*. I brought the scumbag to Harmony, which not only put your safety at risk, but was also one devil of a way to repay this place for how I've been treated."

She shook her head and held on to a calm tone. "Nobody here would blame you."

"I blame me." The corners of his mouth turned down with that stark declaration. "And every day I stick around could be another chance for someone to show up primed to even a score, because Felix Raine wasn't the only creep I've dealt with, trust me. I have to make damn sure that it doesn't happen a second time—not here. Can you understand that?"

Oh, yes. She understood. Better, probably, than he knew. He wasn't only trying to protect her by going, it was also a deliberate effort to keep from further tarnishing the image of a place he considered picture perfect. Her sigh was long and heartfelt. It also held more than a hint of resignation, because she knew what she had to do. Her conscience wouldn't let her not do it.

Jordan Trask thought he didn't deserve to be in some sort of small-town heaven, one that actually existed only in his mind. In reality, what he deserved was the truth. She wasn't surprised that he'd hadn't heard about a certain period in Harmony's history. No one liked to dwell on it. Including her. But that didn't matter, not now.

"I know you think you've somehow spoiled a perfect spot in a far-from-perfect world,'' she said quietly. ''But you're wrong—and I'll tell you why.''

Tess squared her shoulders. ''As awful as a particular part of this Saturday turned out to be, Jordan, it can't compare to a sunny Friday afternoon just over three years ago when two men in their early twenties blew into town, driving a brand-new red convertible they'd hijacked at gunpoint earlier that day in Phoenix. By the time they reached Harmony, they were high as kites on something and apparently set on getting money for more.'' She let the memories come. ''With the element of surprise in their favor, they robbed a couple of gas stations in a matter of minutes, then hit a few other businesses, on the outskirts of the downtown area, and nearly rammed a busload of children on the way home from school before the police could even begin to respond to a crime spree that had sprung up out of nowhere. The bad guys had the upper hand that day.''

She held Jordan's gaze, saw it widening soberly in grim surprise, and staunchly continued. ''Their last stop on the way out of town was a convenience store near the main highway. Things didn't go as smoothly for them there, not when a teenage boy proudly driving his first car pulled up and headed into the store for a soda just as they were cleaning out the cash register. He caught on to what was happening and whirled around to go for help.''

She wouldn't allow her voice to falter. ''That's when they shot him in the back...and put him in a wheelchair.''

''God,'' Jordan said with feeling, blowing out a gusty breath. ''The barber's son.''

''Yes.''

Keeping her gaze steady, Tess forged on. "But that's not the end of it. They stepped right over Brady Crenshaw, ran back to the car they'd stolen and headed down the mountain going far too fast, with two police cars that had just taken up the chase following more cautiously. On a sharp bend in the highway, they lost control of the convertible and skidded over the dividing line. Instants later, they rammed head-on into an oncoming car, which my husband, Roger, was driving." She paused, swallowed. "All three of them died instantly."

Jordan closed his eyes and clenched his jaw. "I had no idea, Tess," he said after a long moment.

"I know."

She wanted to throw her arms around him and just hold on. Instead, she folded them under her breasts. "It's not something people here are eager to talk about, but it's true. For a long time afterward, I kept waiting for something else to happen. I worried about my folks, even nagged them into putting new locks on their doors while I had the same thing done to the house I was living in before I bought theirs. Most of all, though, I worried about Ali. I watched her like a hawk, reluctant to even let her out of my sight, until I realized that smothering her with my concern was no way to raise a happy child."

His eyes opened then, and once again her gaze locked with his. "Bad things happen in the best of places, Jordan. You won't change the reality of that by leaving—or staying."

And was that it, she wondered, running her tongue over her lips. Or should she go on? It didn't take her long to decide. After gearing herself up to give this man the truth, she found she was in the mood for more.

"I don't—and never did—expect you to stay beyond the summer," she said candidly. "I had no doubt that if we became lovers, it would be a temporary affair." *I even wanted it that way,* she thought. "So I know you'll go when you're ready and I'd never try to stop you from leaving. You can trust me on that. But if you let what took place today drive you away, we'll both lose the few weeks we could still have together. And I won't deny I want those weeks... Because I fell in love with you," she added in the next breath, and watched a blankly startled expression form with lightning speed on the face she'd come to know so well. Tess dropped her arms to her sides. "I won't deny that, either. I didn't plan on it, but it happened anyway."

He stared at her, just stared at her, hazel eyes riveted to blue as the wind whipped the air around them. "I don't know what to say," he told her at last.

"Don't say anything, not now. If you decide you want to talk tomorrow, I'll be home."

With that, Tess started for the back door with quick steps, knowing she had to put some distance between them before her hard-won calm deserted her. She needed some time alone, badly. Pushing the door open, she turned and aimed a final solemn look at Jordan.

"Just remember," she said, poised to enter the kitchen and determined to waste no time in letting herself out the front door, "what happens next is up to you. You can be gone in forty-eight hours, or you can wait until you're really ready to leave and get on with your life. Either way, I'll wish you well, believe me.''

She didn't add that a part of her heart would go with him, no matter what.

But she had no doubt that it would.

LONG HOURS LATER, Jordan woke up in a cold sweat. A rowdy storm had blown its way through during the night, but all was silent now as he glanced at the bedside clock and found that it wasn't quite yet five o'clock. Plenty of time for him to go back to sleep. And he wouldn't so much as close his eyes, he knew.

Even if he could manage to drift back into sleep, he wasn't willing to risk having another dream like the one he'd just had, where he'd wandered in a huge garden, exactly as he had more than once in the course of what he'd come to think of as his own personal fantasy. As before, he'd sent himself down a particular bend in the winding path and discovered a woman patiently waiting for him. He could see all of her this time, every inch of her body, every detail of her features, every small movement of her eyes as she'd looked toward him.

But he hadn't been able to reach her. Not tonight. No matter how hard he'd tried, something had kept him from walking into those arms held out in welcome. He'd never felt more alone in his life than he had in the stark moments before he'd surfaced to discover his fingers clenched in a clammy sheet.

Jordan shifted restlessly, finally punched up a pillow and leaned against it. At the movement, the dog stretched out on the rug rose and greeted his master with a quiet woof. Jordan chose to take it as a reminder of the role of man's best friend.

"Okay, pal," he murmured. "I'm not completely alone, because I've got you."

Jones panted out his agreement—and so enthusiastically, it had Jordan's mouth flirting with a smile, the first he'd even come close to achieving since he'd found a slyly smirking part of his past waiting for him. As much as that had jarred him, though, it had taken his lover's sober tale of a time in Harmony's history to totally stun him.

Not here. The words had repeated in his mind as she'd calmly told him about that sunny Friday afternoon when startling events had produced tragic results. *Not here.* But in the end he'd had to admit that his view of things, at least in one particular respect, had been only an illusion.

Harmony wasn't heaven. He knew that now. But that didn't mean it wasn't special. It was. To him, at any rate. And it probably always would be.

So, Trask, are you going...or staying?

Still debating the answer to that one, Jordan got out of bed, pulled on his gray sweats and headed down to the kitchen to make coffee. While it brewed, he let Jones out, closed the door behind both of them and settled himself on the back-porch steps. A cool breeze danced across his bare toes. A fresh, crisp scent rose from the grass below him. To his left, dawn forged its way to life, barely lightening the eastern sky. On his right, an owl hooted in the trees, offering a final tribute to the night.

Memories surfaced, reminding Jordan that in this very spot Frank Fitzgerald had watched the sun set in a blaze of glory more than once with his granddaughter at his side. A family man, Jordan thought. That might well be how he would always think of Frank.

He couldn't deny that he'd learned more on the subject from his houseguest than he ever had from his own father. In fact, he was just beginning to really appreciate how much the big man had taught him.

"Don't get me wrong, pal," Jordan muttered as Jones, having done his duty, dropped down to lounge at his master's feet. "I'm damn glad to have you around. Still, I'm starting to realize that there are a few things missing."

Such as a child to watch the sunset with? he found himself wondering. Right here on these steps, one had kissed his cheek and tried to take his hurts away. He didn't suppose he would ever forget that. Or her. Long after he was gone, the memory would remain.

But when would he go?

Jordan propped his elbows on his knees, knowing he had to figure that one out—and soon—because a woman he cared about beyond any he'd ever known deserved a clear-cut answer. As far as he was concerned, no one deserved it more. Here, inches from where he now sat, she had told him she loved him, and so candidly that he didn't doubt it for a second, even though that particular emotion had been stranger to him for much of his life.

She loved him. Certain of that, could he leave her in a matter of hours?

No.

The word rang in his mind, loud and clear enough to have him recognizing it as the sheer truth, one he couldn't escape any more than he'd been able to escape his past. Jordan didn't even bother to try, accepting the blunt fact that at the moment not much would stand a chance of dragging him away. He simply couldn't leave, not yet.

So he was staying.

With that conclusion reached, the muscle-tight tension that had helped keep him up throughout much of the night began to ease, but before he could even roll his shoulders in relief, another thought struck.

Did he want to leave...ever?

No!

It was a silent shout ripping through him this time. Jordan's gaze widened in a flash as its meaning hit home, hard. Just like that, he knew.

"I don't want to leave at all," he muttered out loud, looking straight ahead and seeing far more than the quiet scene before him. "In fact, I flat out can't leave, not now, because I don't just care about Tess Cameron. It's more than that—a helluva lot more—" he shook his head "— and I've been a downright fool not to realize it before."

Jones wasted no time in responding to that news with a short snort. Steps above him, his master had little troubling deciding what that meant.

"Okay," Jordan said ruefully, dropping his gaze and blowing out a breath, "so we agree that I haven't been very swift on the uptake. What I could really use at the moment, though, is some help. I don't suppose you've got any suggestions as to how I'm going to make a living in this place."

Jones just blinked dark eyes and yawned widely.

Jordan released another breath, thinking that he could probably use a cup of coffee to jump-start his brain before he tackled that problem. He had to tackle it, that was for sure, because he wasn't going to tell Tess how he felt until he had a definite game plan when it came to a job. Some might call it pride—or pure stubborn male ego—but that's the way it was.

Intent on heading back to the kitchen for a fortifying dose of caffeine, Jordan edged himself around toward one side of the steps—only to freeze in midmotion as the first watery rays of a very early sun suddenly slanted over the horizon and landed on a sight that had him frankly staring.

There were tomatoes growing in his yard.

Against all odds, two of them—tiny yet unmistakably visible greenish globes—had bloomed to life on a thin branch that bore its burden with no sign of any drooping, not today. A group of new leaves had sprouted as well, and they looked healthy, not wilted. The whole plant, in fact, as small as it still was, seemed to be standing straighter and taller, as though proud of its achievement.

"And you should be, buddy," Jordan murmured, carefully leaning over to touch a narrow stem with the barest brush of long fingers. "You did it, bless you. You came through and proved the experts wrong."

And this is right. The right job for you, Trask.

Jordan blinked, firmly set back on his heels by that thought. An ex Border Patrol agent who still hardly knew one flower from another, who didn't have a lick of formal education when it came to plants, turning gardener? For a *living?*

Ridiculous, was all he could conclude, knowing full well that jaws would drop all over the place if he so much as mentioned the idea to his former colleagues. And that was before the round of chuckles started. But then, their job was no longer his job, he reminded himself, and it never would be. Not again. He was positive on that score. So if a future carved out of rich, black soil was what would suit him best at this point in his life, they were welcome to laugh all they wanted.

But would it suit him? After several thoughtful minutes, he found himself nodding slowly as the notion settled in. Who would have figured that weeks of mulling over the issue of what to do next career-wise would all boil down to this? Not him, certainly. But it had, he had to admit. Somehow, some way, it did seem as if this was the kind of work to pin his future on—the challenge of making things grow.

So he would.

With that decision made, his spirits took a rapid turn for the better. All at once he wanted to not only laugh but roar, loud enough to wake up the whole neighborhood. And maybe launch into a sadly off-key tune, something he normally reserved for the shower, just for the hell of it. Most of all, though, he wanted to see Tess. Badly.

Jordan turned and aimed a look at the house next door, one he'd come to feel even more at home in than the homey place he'd rented. There, he discovered that a kitchen light had been switched on sometime during the past few minutes, painting the windows with a golden glow. His lips quickly curved at the sight. Tess clearly wasn't having any better luck at sleeping than he'd had. He supposed a sensitive man could work up some sympathy in response to that fact, but at the moment he was feeling too damn good to even try.

He rose to his bare feet, bent when he reached the bottom of the steps and gave the dog a brief pat. "I'll be back later, pal. Right now, I have to see a blue-eyed woman about the rest of my life."

Spurred on by a lively bark, Jordan raced to the

slatted fence and scaled it in one swift motion. He was more than ready to share several things with Tess, and he knew exactly where he wanted to do it.

It wasn't in the kitchen...or the bedroom.

SHE HAD JUST POURED boiling water into the teapot when a brisk knock sounded on the back door. Tess had little doubt as to who it was. She'd been up a good part of the night thinking about him, wondering how long it would be before she had to say goodbye. Hours or weeks? Maybe neither, she now had to concede. If he'd come to bid her farewell, it might be minutes.

Hoping for the best yet braced for the worst, she crossed the room in the fuzzy slippers that matched the buttercup-yellow of her terry-cloth robe and pushed the sheer ivory curtain covering the glass half of the door aside. A devilishly sexy grin was the first thing she saw. It took her less than a second to decide what it meant.

Yes! She would have him for *weeks.*

Resisting the urge to whoop, she let the curtain drop and flung the door open. Then she launched herself straight at her lover. "Good morning," she said as she landed flat against him. Because all at once it was.

"Morning." Jordan's arms quickly wrapped around her. "I have a lot to tell you," he murmured in her ear, holding her close. And with that, he swept her right off her feet, carrying her with ease as he switched around and started for the yard.

Her brows made a fast climb. "Are we going for a walk?"

"Uh-huh."

"Where?"

"You'll see."

And she did. She just couldn't quite believe it when he stopped by the flower bed in full summer bloom at the side of her house and plopped down on the grass, settling her into his lap. Thank goodness she'd put on her robe, was all she could think. Otherwise, she might have been carried off wearing only her nightgown, and under a sky that was steadily getting brighter. Certainly it was light enough to make out the determined set of a chiseled jaw displaying a night's growth of dark stubble. Attractive? Absolutely. Still she wasn't eager for anyone else to get a glimpse of that sight at the moment.

Tess ran her tongue over her lips. "Don't you think we should go back into the house?"

"Later," Jordan said, his voice low yet firm. "First, I figured we should talk about a few things right where it all started." He leaned back slightly for a short study. "Fortunately, you don't look like you're in the mood to strangle anybody today."

It made her smile. "That's because my flowers haven't been trampled lately."

"Hold that thought," he told her, "because while you're in a friendly frame of mind, I have some news to pass along."

"I already know," she quickly countered, sure of what she was about to say. "You'll be staying here for the rest of the summer."

"Not exactly."

Her hands clenched on his shoulders as her stomach started to take a quick dive.

"Actually," he went on in the next breath, looking

her straight in the eye, "I just plan on staying. Period."

Now she had to gape. Unless her ears had deceived her, the man had said that he intended to stay in Harmony—permanently. And while she might have questioned her hearing, it was impossible to doubt the steely cast of his steady gaze. He planned to stay, all right. Period.

Say something, Tess, she ordered herself as the silence between them built. But she couldn't, not yet.

"I suppose I should clarify that statement," Jordan said at last.

She managed to dip her head in a nod.

"Right." He released a short breath. "I guess I'll start with the tomatoes."

"Tomatoes," she repeated cautiously, totally at sea.

"I just found two little ones sprouting on that plant everyone shook their heads over."

Her response came easily this time. "That's wonderful," she said, and fully meant it, because she knew how much that discovery would mean to him.

"I intend to see more of them, too," he added. "With any luck, I'll see a whole bunch more—because I'm pretty well set on trying my hand at growing a variety of things." He paused for a beat. "Which is why I'm hoping you'll look kindly on letting me become partners with you."

Tess was still at sea, until her brain caught up. "In the *landscaping* business," she said.

"You got it."

She could only wonder if she were dreaming. But he felt very real everywhere they touched, strong and solid. "Jordan, are you truly serious about this?"

"Yes," he said. "I'll admit I have a lot to learn, but I'm also willing to put a lot into it, including a good chunk of my savings. When the Zieglers are ready to sell their business, I want both of us to sign on the dotted line under Buyer."

"Partners." She murmured the word, tasting it on her tongue. "Cameron and Trask Landscaping."

His gaze didn't waver. "I was thinking more along the lines of *Trasks* Landscaping, as in two people."

Tess was back to gaping. "As in a couple?" she asked very carefully.

Hazel eyes lit with something she'd never quite seen in them before. "As in marriage."

Marriage. The word echoed through her. Only weeks earlier, she'd been of no mind to take another walk down the aisle. But that, Tess thought, was before she'd tumbled heart first for this man. Still her prior experience urged caution.

"Jordan, I have to think about this. There's Ali to consider and—"

"And I want her as a definite part of this package," he said, breaking in. "Actually, I have a hunch she'd be pleased as punch if we got together."

Tess couldn't argue with that, not when her daughter's recent departing words had been, *Bake Mr. T a pie sometime, would you, Mom? Maybe you could help him eat it, too, and go out with him for pizza, if he asks you. He might be kinda lonely with just Jones for company.*

"She probably would be pleased," Tess confessed. It wouldn't surprise her if Ali had decided to try her hand at matchmaking. Sally, Tess thought fleetingly, would be proud.

"I know I can't replace Ali's father." Jordan's expression sobered with that statement. ''Still, instead of her calling me Mr. T, or even Jordan, what I'd really like, if she'd like it, is for her to call me...Dad.''

A sudden tear formed and slipped down Tess's cheek without warning at that last word. *Dad.* She hadn't been able to cry, either the afternoon before, when she'd been trying mightily to produce a few convincing tears as part of her act, or during endless hours spent staring into the darkness last night, when she'd faced the all-too-real possibility of having to let this man go much too soon. Now Tess found herself on the verge of bawling like a baby.

''Jordan, I suspect Ali would like that, too, but...''

''But I haven't told you yet that I've finally figured out I love you.'' The man who held her muttered what sounded like a self-directed curse under his breath, chewing himself out. ''Jeez, no wonder you're hesitating.''

Now she had to hug him, long and hard. The tears retreated as a soft smile edged her mouth. ''I thought you probably did, since you mentioned marriage, but there's no substitute for hearing the words.''

''All right. I love you.''

''Good. I love you, too.''

''But you still haven't said yes,'' he reminded her when she pulled back and once again met his gaze. ''You know, it's hard to get down on one knee with you in my lap.''

Most of her had come around to the idea of saying yes, she couldn't deny. Larger-than-life men could, she'd found, be very persuasive, but the last dregs of caution remained. Another man had made her his wife only to come to the conclusion that the sort of life she knew so suited her wasn't what he really desired for himself.

"I'll give you a break and pass on the traditional kneeling," she told Jordan, sniffing away the last trace of tears. "There's one thing I have to be very sure of, though." She drew in a breath. "Will you honestly and truly be content to live life in the slow lane?"

He didn't ask what she meant. And he didn't answer immediately. But when the words eventually came they were solemn and straightforward.

"The fast lane may be fine for one person," he told her, "or maybe even two people who want to share that piece of the road. But it's not wide enough, not nearly, to hold a family traveling side by side. And that's what I want more than anything—to be a part of a real family. Give me the chance to do that, Tess, and I'll be more than content with it, believe me."

She did. How could she not? she wondered. Looking into the clear depths of his eyes and finding the truth starkly reflected there, right at the core of him, she and her heart simply had to believe.

"In that case," she murmured, reaching up to gently stroke her fingers over a beard-roughened jaw still taut with determination, "I'm saying *yes*."

He sighed, heavily. "Well, it's about time, lady. You had my gut tied in knots."

"I'm sorry." But she couldn't help smiling.

"You should be." All at once his gaze lit again, this time with a very familiar gleam. "But now that we've got everything settled..."

"Jordan, we can't," she informed him in no uncertain terms even as he lowered her to the grass. ''The neighbors could be up any minute.''

The temporary lover she'd been set on taking, one she now believed would make even better husband material, grinned his sexiest grin. ''Then we'll just have to hurry, won't we?''

* * * * *

Come back to HARMONY this September when Sharon Swan pens another heartwarming tale for Harlequin American Romance.